ISBN: 978-1-989206-33-1

# THE

# MIDNIGHT

# EXHIBIT

Volume 1

his notebook or do homework. If you didn't pay proper attention, that put you in the suspect pool, didn't it?

The detective wasn't from their town, was just the detective who worked for the Sheriff's or something, which covered the whole county, but still: a detective. That was a step up.

For Bryan's disappearance it had just been Principal Masterton at the front of the auditorium, and for Derek M's it had been two cops, both of whom maybe talked fine into the handheld mic of their patrol cars, but pretty much sucked at not popping and spitting into the big microphone.

Still the detective's presentation was the same as the two cops', pretty much, which had been the same as Masterson's, which Roster could have listed out on scratch paper without ever even going to Assembly:

- When's the last you saw Bryan/Derek M/Lorelei?
- What do Bryan/Derek M/Lorelei usually do after school?
- Had anybody unusual been hanging around the high school parking lot, or the adjacent church parking lot, or maybe the graveyard behind the church?

- Does anybody have any notes or letters from Bryan/Derek M/Lorelei?
- Do (note the present tense) Bryan/Derek M/Lorelei play D&D, or anything Satanic or devil-related
- Do Bryan/Derek M/Lorelei have any enemies?
- Has anything important about Bryan/Derek M/Lorelei been written or scratched into any of the bathroom stalls?

Roster—real name "Ross," at least until eighth grade when he got cut from the football roster, most likely due to the color of his hair at the time—didn't go to the cafeteria for any anonymous one-on-one with the detective, but that was just because the last time he'd seen Lorelei hadn't even been an actual interaction, and had probably been a bit leery.

She'd been standing outside Chemistry, in her usual gaggle of cheerleader airheads. The perkiness level practically made the air hazy with glitter. Roster just ducked his head to push through, get to Algebra, but then a flurry of motion at the center of their group caught his attention.

His first thought, *pre*-thought really, as it just happened without his say-so, was that they'd smuggled an injured bird in from the parking lot. Except these weren't exactly the girls who would stoop to touch a dying gross thing.

Roster had slowed, risked a look into their circle.

What Lorelei had, what was keeping them all fascinated...Roster hadn't seen one since junior high, he was pretty sure. Maybe even elementary.

It was one of those fortune-teller things that you made with folding paper this way and that, like you were making an airplane, except then you went further, into origami-land, ended up with a contraption you could cram each of your hands' middle and index fingers into to open and close like a flower. They usually had colors and numbers written on them, he remembered, and then some secret name or fortune or doom written deep inside them, which you always had to shake your head no about, that *that* couldn't be true, no way.

Why the varsity cheerleading squad would be into something junior high like that, Roster had zero idea, and didn't much care, either: just past that switchpicker-thing had been Lorelei's chest, and not only did she look up at precisely the right moment to catch him perving out on her, Stedman the linebacker had as well. At which point, because high school is what it is, he steered Roster into the bathroom, laid down the usual threats and then sealed them by taking Roster's backpack hostage for the day—the backpack which had Roster's Algebra homework, Algebra being the main subject he was for sure failing if he had one more late assignment.

It wasn't exactly a story that the detective in the cafeteria needed to hear, Roster was pretty sure.

And besides, he knew he didn't have anything to do with Lorelei's disappearance, or Bryan's, or Derek M's, so it's not like keeping his big confession to himself about his last interact with her was exactly stalling the investigation out or anything, right?

Right.

Instead of taking the bus home, he strategically missed it, only sulked out when the coast was clear, to walk the ditch the half-mile to his house.

His backpack didn't smell like pee anymore, so that was good. Either that or he was getting used to it.

And Mr. Gonzales *was*, for once in the history of the known world, letting him turn his Algebra in late, no points off.

Roster shook the bright purple bangs out of his

eyes, did his lips in what he considered a punk sneer, cut his eyes down to slits, and stalked through the dry grass, kicking every stray cup and bag he came across, at least until that felt petty, like what a kid would do. Or would that be petulant? Was that the same thing?

Roster shook his head again, to clear it of exactly those kind of stupid, beat-my-ass pee-on-my-backpack thoughts. Nobody cared about the shades of difference between *petty* and *petulant*, and whether they were related, ran into each other at the family reunion or whatever.

This made Roster snicker, but he hid that under his hand fast, on instinct.

The world, he knew, was a wall of linebackers, pretty much, and Roster was always just looking down to realize he had what they wanted.

Still, "Hope you're all right," he muttered to the idea of Lorelei.

They'd sort of been friends in fifth grade, when she'd still lived across the street.

It wasn't her fault she looked like she did, which ended up sucking her into the class of people that preyed on the Bright Hairs. The Unusually-Coifed. The Rainbow-Headed.

The name was still a work in progress.

Roster grinned, then scanned around for if

13

anybody'd seen.

He was all alone, as usual.

He cocked his foot back to kick the next Styrofoam cup, then remembered he was in high school, not elementary, so made like this was just a fancy step, an extra long step, was exactly what anybody cool would have done.

It wasn't a cup anyway.

It was Lorelei's switchpicker thing.

—

In his room off the garage—it was meant to be a storage closet, but Roster had talked his mom into it—Roster inspected his find.

Some kid had spent some serious time on this.

Every panel—eleven by his count, which didn't make symmetrical kind of sense for an origami-thing with four parts—was covered with the finest ink. Like, calligraphy, or Spirograph, something dense like an engineer or an architect might do in a meeting, or while watching a movie he didn't really want to watch. Roster was only basing that on guys her mom had tried out over the last few years, but it felt right.

And, instead of numbers or colors, all the choices written in a kind of elvish script were...fountain drinks?

Yep: Coke, Pepsi, Pibb, and Sprite were the

first four.

The eight that those opened up to were actors' names: Molly, Tom, Rob, Judd, Johnny, Winona, Alyssa, Ally.

This was less a fortune, more like the video shelf at the gas station. Roster processed through it—not like anyone was watching, right?

When he unfolded the secret panel under *Pepsi* and *Alyssa*, what he got then was a number: 6.

"What?" he said.

Numbers were usually the top stage, the first round, not the big secret at the end.

Not bothering to process through some different *Pepsi/Judd*-path, he unfolded the rest of the panels.

The first was blank, and the second was too—this switchpicker had four at the end instead of eight, which meant two names opened onto each surprise—but then the third...it didn't open at first, and when it did.

Was that gum?

Roster dropped the thing, came back with the eraser ends of two pencils scrounged from his desk drawer, because for all he knew this was jock-saliva.

The gooey panel lifted, the gum stretching, stringing...finally letting go.

15

Not gum, no.

It was like someone had trapped a cricket in there, squished it. A big squishy cricket.

Roster gagged—it was his superpower, pretty much—pushed the whole thing away, and hid in *Hardcastle and McCormick* with his mom, over leftover lasagne that was crunchy where it had dried out, and by the time he got back to his room, the fresh-beige of whatever that had been on the switchpicker, it was crusted over black.

Instead of dropping it into his trash, Roster scooped the switchpicker into the turned-sideway can, then hand-delivered it to the barrel they kept by the utility pole in the front yard by the street. The brick was still on the round lid, which meant his mom had taken the trash out, not him, like she'd told him to.

"Shit," he said. He'd really meant to do that this time. *And* to remember, for once, to put the brick on the lid.

Maybe tomorrow, he told himself. Definitely tomorrow.

He tumped the trash in, hiding three crunchy socks as well, and then, slouching back up the driveway, he realized something was wrong.

It took him a moment, but then he got it: the house across the street's front bedroom light had a little bit of glow to it.

Since Lorelei's family had been black-molded from it months ago, it had been empty, abandoned.

Roster stood there, considering this development.

"Detective?" he said. "I think I know where she is, maybe."

—

Lying in bed with his walkman two hours later, he realized that his fingers weren't dancing with the song, they were pointed like they were stuffed up into the sharp points of Lorelei's switchpicker, and there were going back and forth, like trying to find a different path down into the secret panels. Faster and faster, the music ramping up in his head.

Roster ripped his headphones off, sat up in bed.

His mom was already either asleep or watching her little TV with the sound off—same thing—so Roster didn't have anybody to ask about this. Not that he would have.

*Um, Mom? What if my fingers still feel like they're inside a dead girl's last toy?*

Yeah, try that.

Instead, Roster dialed his brain up to eleven on a pile of notebook paper, folded every which way until he stumbled into the right pattern to make the crappiest switchpicker ever. It was really just a series of airplane noses, doubled over twice. His idea was that knowing the inner workings of one of them would make it not weird anymore—would let his fingers forget what it had felt like, and stop trying to do it more.

The action on his wasn't as crisp as Lorelei's had been, but he wrote that off as just him not being a fourth grade girl. Or, if Lorelei had actually made this one, then not being a seventeen-year-old girl, who cares.

Roster crumpled it into a stupid ball, left it on his stupid desk.

Directly in front of him, just across the street, Lorelei's light was still on.

"Such absolute bullshit," he said to himself.

To prove to himself what bullshit it had to be, he pulled his clothes back on, crept down the hall and out the front door.

For what he knew was too long, he stood by the trash can, watching Lorelei's black-mold house. Specifically, he stood there long enough that he could hear something rooting through the trash, never mind that the brick was definitely still there on the lid.

"Baby raccoon," he finally decided out loud.

A raccoon family had been scavenging, and one had got left behind, couldn't push that lid up.

What else could it be, right? No bird could get in there, no snake could get in there. A big roach, maybe, or a swarm of them, or a crawling mass of maggots birthed up from scrambled eggs and the chicken that had gone bad last week. All of the above, maybe.

Roster smiled.

It was getting so gross he kind of *had* to look.

Shielding his face from the chance of flies, he popped the lid off, already leaning away.

Nothing.

He felt on the ground behind him for a rock, lobbed it in, half-hoping a baby raccoon was going to launch up, half-praying that wouldn't happen, as he'd probably piss himself.

Again, nothing.

Finally Roster leaned over fast, not so much looking as giving anything in there a glimpse of his face, and when nothing scrabbled out in an animal panic, he finally just pushed the trash over.

It spilled across the sidewalk, out into the street.

"Just garbage," Roster muttered.

He checked Lorelei's window. It was still glowing.

Because she might be watching, he faked like he was brave enough to wade into that trash, kick it around for an answer to the clicking, the scratching, the *sound*.

There was nothing. Just, farthest away from the actual muck, that fancy switchpicker.

It was whole again, wasn't crumpled anymore, had evidently been made well enough to shrug back into its intended shape.

"Well," Roster said, and toed it farther away from the black hole of the trash can, far enough he could finally pick it up.

The fingers of his right hand fell into their place, ready to play again.

Roster looked down, promised himself to play with whatever fountain drink first came to mind, or memory, whatever, and, on the way to thinking that, he remembered how these things were supposed to work: each of the initial four panels were supposed to have *different* numbers of letters to their words, to land you on a different inner panel, right?

But *Coke* and *Pibb* each had four, didn't they? Like...was it like, since *two* of the four options would lead you in, then that was the right way? But wouldn't they each open onto different actors?

It didn't make sense.

"Coke," Roster said all the same, and looked down, leaned the switchpicker over to make that selection.

*Bryan* looked back up at him. Not Molly Ringwold or Tom Cruise, not stupid Rob Lowe or Johnny pouts-a-lot Depp, not Judd Nelson, not Johnny—who was that, anyway?—and not Winona Ryder or Ally Sheedy. Not even his trusty Alyssa Milano.

Bryan. As in, Bryan Simms, the kid they'd had Assembly about, since nobody knew where he was.

Roster stepped back without looking, caught the curb with his heel and splatted onto his ass, nearly fumbling the switchpicker away.

The next panel was—he should have known—was *DM*, for "Derek M." Shaking his head no but unfolding anyway, next was *Lorelei*.

Last was *Ross*. As in, the kid still hiding under the stupid name he never even wanted.

"Bullshit," Roster said. He tried to shake the switchpicker off but it clung to his fingers, was gooey inside now. Roster pinched with his right hand, got his left free—*was that blood?*—and, in the snapshot his eyes took before he shook his left free, the switchpicker had opened to the next option, the one that wasn't ready for him to be seeing it yet: *hrs*.

Roster pushed back and back, onto the lawn he still hadn't mowed.

"Hours?" he said, his voice too loud for night, he knew.

Nobody was out here with him, though.

Hours, though?

Roster stood then bent back over to clean his hands on the tall damp grass.

He looked for the bright flash of the switchpicker but—

"Baby raccoon stole it," he told the imaginary detective, forcing a smile.

He was holding his left hand like it was injured, but it wasn't. He studied it.

There was no trash goo on it. No melted candy. No blood.

He looked back to his house, hoping his mom would be standing in the doorway, to call him back in.

"I'm out here," he said, when she wasn't there.

He made himself step back onto the sidewalk, still holding his unhurt hand.

"Six," he told himself.

It was the only other secret the switchpicker had whispered to him, until now.

"Six *hours*?" he asked it.

He narrowed his eyes to dial back to when he'd

gone down into those inner panels for the first time.

Four o'clock or so?

And it was, what, nine-thirty now?

"Five and a half hours later..." he heard himself saying, and when he looked up and down the street, the lights flickering like they probably always had been, what he imagined was a giant switchpicker turned upside, its points legs, so it could take huge ponderous steps closer and closer to him.

Roster shook his head, clearing it of that stupid possibility.

He wasn't scared of Stedman, and he wasn't going to let this spook him either. He wasn't a kid anymore.

He stepped down from the curb, crunched through the trash, and crossed the street.

—

Swishing through the dead grass of Lorelei's old house, Roster stopped, turned his head to the side, and, and: what if the switchpicker was upside down? What if you looked at it from the bottom, not the top, right? Could things also be written on the panels you were only supposed to touch, never actually see? Like, could you be calling a spell down on yourself or something, never even know it?

23

Probably, he figured. Especially with a switchpicker somebody's spent that much time on.

But, too, he told himself, he was just thinking of reasons to turn around, not go to Lorelei's window.

He breathed in, made himself push through those dead shrubs.

Like always, he couldn't see anything. Her posters were still taped two- and three-deep to the glass.

"Figures," Roster said, not for the first time.

Why would she be hiding out in her old bedroom, though? That was what he wanted to know. Her life, her everything—she had it made, didn't she? Why would a cheerleader with a jock boyfriend run away, camp out in her black-mold house?

Roster knocked lightly on the glass and the light in the bedroom wavered a bit, like it was from a lantern maybe, and a body had just crossed in front of it.

Ten seconds later, just long enough to have hustled down the hall, the front door opened, its hinges a creaky invitation.

Roster looked across the street for his mom again. Again, she wasn't there.

He tightroped behind the bushes to the porch,

stood in the black doorway.

"Lori?" he called into the darkness of the living room.

No answer.

Was she poised by the sliding door across the living room, ready to blast out into the night if he had the detective with him?

What was she running from?

"Lorelei?" he said then, her high school name.

Nothing.

He stepped over the threshold, telling himself that wasn't a gulp in his throat.

The house smelled like wet and rot and worse. On the wall something glinted—a built-in mirror, yeah. It had always been there.

Roster kept his hand to the damp right wall and followed it to the hall.

The light from Lorelei's old bedroom was spilling out onto the rancid carpet.

He called her name again, and added that his mom was waiting for him.

No response.

"Such bullshit," Roster hissed to himself, and then jerked his hand away when the fingertip of his middle finger caught a nail or something.

It came back not hot and hurting but cold and numb, and not even bleeding. Just...open?

He looked at it as well as he could in the non-light, then inserted it into his mouth, took another step, another step, and then—

He pulled his hand hard from his face but there was a string of heat going from the new hole in his fingertip, straight down his throat. Something wriggling, alive.

He watched it pull in half, one part retracting into his finger, the other half diving down his throat.

He bent over, gagged from deeper than he ever had, but the puke, for once, wouldn't come. It felt like his face was bulging from the effort, like his eyeballs were going to burst out onto his cheeks, hang by their stalks.

His hands were in the carpet and it was mushy and cold.

"What—what—?" he managed to say, and when he looked up, Lorelei was standing in the glowing doorway of her old bedroom.

She was wearing her cheerleading outfit, the sweater vest part just as tight as ever.

"Ross," she said, just an identification.

Her pigtails were so bubbly.

She'd picked *Winona*, Roster knew.

If that had even been what the switchpicker had shown her.

"It's different for each of us, isn't it?" he said up to her.

"Silly," she said, and canted her head into the forbidden space of her bedroom, held her hand out sideways to pull him in.

Roster stood up, was still unsteady enough that he fell into the soggy wall, left a shoulder impression there.

"Don't worry about that," Lorelei said, and that was when Roster saw that the print on the raised fabric of the "D" of her cheer top, it was that same fine scrollwork the switchpicker had been lined with. Like graph paper, but a hundred times denser. A thousand. And not square, but like the texture of some larger design.

"I—I can't, my mom—" Roster said, stepping away, but now there was a sound behind him.

He spun, and in the blackness of the living room, there was—

But it couldn't be.

A single giant point—*leg*—of the upside-down switchpicker. Meaning, to accommodate that, the living room, it must be vast, warehouse-big.

Roster was breathing hard now.

"Better hurry," Lorelei said.

"Why?" Roster said.

"Because it takes four, of course," Lorelei said,

and stepped back into the depths of her bedroom.

Roster looked behind again, to see if he could make it past that leg, past that maw clicking far above that had to be like an octopus beak, just, one made from paper, but it was like the force of his looking collapsed the giant switchpicker into confetti.

No, not confetti.

A thousand little versions of itself, all crawling like spiders.

Roster flinched back, caught himself on the wall, the wet wallpaper and sheetrock tearing away, and he backed away more, and more, the paper things on the wall now, and coating the carpet toward him.

He fell into Lorelei's bedroom.

"I don't—I don't—" he said, his breath deep, his face hot and cold at the same time.

"Like what you saw?" Lorelei said without looking up to him from her seated place on the floor, and...and that was exactly what Stedman had hissed into Roster's ear in the bathroom. Right after he'd caught Roster checking out his girlfriend's chest.

Or maybe she was talking about him, Roster, being the original reason she'd papered her bedroom window with posters.

Had the black mold this house had got infected with been the residue of all the nights he'd spent trying to catch a glimpse?

It had just been innocent, though, he wanted to argue. No harm, no foul. You, Lorelei, never even had to know.

But that day in the hall before she disappeared, she had looked up over the switchpicker, caught him at last.

And—had she looked up because the panel she'd just unfolded had told her to?

It could change like that, Roster knew.

It wasn't a normal little bullshit toy, made by a fourth-grader with too much time on her hands. It was...if it hadn't been a switchpicker, it would have been a Magic 8-Ball, it would have been a Rubik's Cube, it would have been the backwards lyrics on a record.

It had been waiting for him, too. And not *just* him.

"I just wanted to play, man," Derek M said, sitting across from Lorelei, and without even meaning to, Roster remembered Derek M scratching unmentionable things into the metal of the bathroom stalls, and then drawing an anatomically-correct picture beside those things.

"Hey, dude," Bryan said, the most decomposed

29

of them all—Roster could see now that Derek M's lips were mostly gone, like he'd been chewing them. And there were black veins in Lorelei's bare legs. But Bryan's skin was all sloughing down, and off.

"Hey," Roster said to him, trying not to look too hard.

Bryan Simms, he of the famous photo he'd mimeographed into a flier, and stapled onto every bulletin board in school for about five minutes.

It was long enough, though.

"What about you?" Roster said to Lorelei.

"Everybody's got something," she said with a shrug, dismissing the question, the confession, but Roster knew the rumor about her and Mr. Gonzales, that, first, had turned out to be made-up, but, second, had, he guessed now, been started by Lorelei herself. Maybe because Mr. Gonzales didn't allow late work. Or, he didn't then, anyway.

It didn't matter anymore.

"Your turn," Bryan said, offering up the fourth seat of their circle, and, after checking the doorway—empty, no paper spiders—Roster settled down.

Lorelei did too, and Roster's eyes automatically flashed to her legs, her skirt.

"Sorry," he said, trying not to look anywhere

else.

"Still the same," she said to him, and then she reached forward, between them, not for the switchpicker—that was for kids—but the bottle. That was what they were playing now, then. That was what the game had become.

She spun the bottle on its side and Derek M grinned with the thrill of it, and when it landed on Bryan, he nodded to himself like for strength, made himself breathe in and out fast and deep, then drew the bottle up all at once, turned it up, drank a long drink.

When he pulled away, Roster saw a black shiny aliveness slurping between his mouth and the bottle, and Bryan, coughing hard, the eyehole of his face skin down around his cheek now, held the bottle ahead, for whoever was next.

Lorelei took it, set it back down on its side between them, and Bryan's cough finally produced a dark sheen on his chin, and a new hollowness in the one of his eyes still lined up.

"This is *fun*," Derek M said, grinning wide, his teeth broken and rotted, and Lorelei spun the bottle again, and Roster watched it, his heart swelling in chest, because soon it would be his turn, he knew.

¤

"He's not answering!" Eleonore shouted, holding her phone tight to her face. "It's only midnight, why isn't he answering?" She'd dialed Ross' cellphone the moment the driver finished his story. The way the Ross in the story acted...she could see her boy.

"Cool it," Tobias said, eyes pinned out his window.

They'd come to a stop at a light. The door of a dive bar swung open and three women in short skirts and high boots stepped out. One of them waved at Tobias.

"Aren't you listening? Aren't you worried?" Eleonore said, her voice was high and bird-like with panic.

"He's fine...but not as fine as those sluts." Tobias had whispered the second bit.

"What?"

"Nothing. Say, how much surgery would it take for you to look that fine again?"

Eleonore scrunched her face tight. "You're drunk."

"You're old."

"I'm four years younger than you. Just because

men get to age—"

The driver slammed the shifter and the truck jerked when the light changed. "I knew a handsome man who worked in tall buildings and took what he wanted, used women up."

"Let me guess, his name was Ross, no wait, was it Tobias?" Tobias craned his neck to gawk longer at the young women.

"His name was Joe. Joe had a way with women."

"Got that pussy, huh?" Tobias said, decidedly tired of riding in the stuffy cab with this huge bozo in monster paint.

Eleonore shook her head. "I hate when you get like this."

"Joe got all that he deserved," the driver said and shifted to second.

# ANOTHER PRETTY FACE

## Renee Miller

Joe stood, grabbed his briefcase and then his keys, and walked toward the door. She waited outside, face flushed, arms unsure where to put themselves. He liked knowing he made people nervous.

33

"You ready?" he asked.

She nodded. "Yes, but I'm not sure why you—"

"To make amends," he said. "I told you I never wanted to make you feel uncomfortable. Let me make things good. We can start over. Right foot, blah, blah."

"It's fine. Really."

"No, it's not." Joe nudged her toward the elevators. "I just have a client meeting, which you can help with, and then it's dinner anywhere you want."

"Thank you, sir."

"Call me Joe, Sherry. We've been through enough to be friends now, haven't we?"

She nodded.

"Come on then. We're going to be late."

Joe led the way to the elevators. Sherry followed, as he knew she would. He smiled as she pressed herself in the far corner of the elevator, making herself appear small and vulnerable. The woman was a shark, though. She'd played a complex game that almost got him in the end.

They never said no to him for long. Male or female, Joe always managed to get his way, both in the office and in the bedroom. Part of it was his physical appeal. He knew he was exceptionally attractive. Learned that early in life and used it to his advantage whenever possible. Combined with his confidence, his sharp mind and cutting wit, he was almost irresistible.

Now and then, though, he came across someone like Sherry, who played the game a little too long, and he had to end it before things got ridiculous.

As they left the building, Joe hailed a cab.

"I'll just take my car," Sherry said. "I can meet you there."

"Nonsense," Joe scoffed. "We'll ride together to the meeting. I can have the service bring your car when you decide on a restaurant."

She hesitated as a cab pulled up to the curb. "Don't let the dark in," she said.

"I'm sorry?"

After quick look back at the building, Sherry clutched her bag tightly to her chest. "Nothing." She ducked into the cab. Joe followed and gave the driver the hotel address. This would be worth every second of torture Sherry heaped on him. He wondered how long she'd pretend to be the innocent virgin. Probably right until she came.

—

Joe strolled down the hallway, smoothing his shirt, satisfied with the night's events. He'd pursued Sherry for weeks. She probably thought she could string him along forever, but he set her straight. Bitch could barely move now. He'd have to fire her, though, or she'd get uppity. They always did.

She'd only gotten the job because she was nice to look at. In truth, she was a terrible assistant. She lost files, misdirected phone calls, got agitated when he touched her arm or her shoulder. Hell, he could barely walk past her desk without her practically jumping out of her skin. She'd gone to H.R. after a couple of weeks and said he was harassing her. They knew the deal. She wasn't the first, nor would she be the last to think she was special.

He told H.R. she was upset because he wasn't playing her game. He was a partner, for crying out loud, and partners didn't chase anyone. They offered mediation. He accepted. Sherry calmed down after a couple of sessions. He was contrite, apologetic, and their mediator clearly took his side.

She needed the job. He knew it. She knew it. They agreed to continue their work relationship, and he offered to take her out for dinner to make amends. Just like she wanted, although, once upstairs, she started acting weird. Played the frightened virgin the second she realized there were no clients waiting for them in the room.

Christ, he hated that tactic. Why can't a

woman just admit she likes sex? Was it so hard? Had to make him the bad guy every time.

He took his phone from his pocket, scrolled to Matthew's number and pressed call. "Matt?"

"It's two in the fucking morning, Joe," Matt said.

"Sorry, but I just made a decision about Sherry."

A sigh.

"I tried to make it work, man, but she's still fucking up. The whole harassment thing is off the table, so don't worry about it. She just can't do the job and we shouldn't have to keep her on just to avoid a bit of bad press."

"You finished mediation? Tried to smooth it over?"

"We went out tonight to bury the hatchet. She can't have done the things she did and still say I'm harassing her, if you know what I mean."

"You dog!" Matt laughed. "Beat her at her own game, eh?"

"Fucking right. No point in keeping her on."

"Ellie will be upset if she tells anyone she fucked you."

"Ellie knows how lucky she is. She'll believe what I tell her to believe. I'm not worried."

"Okay. I'll write her pink slip in the morning.

Better I deal with her than you."

"That's what I thought."

"You giving her a reason for termination?"

Joe pressed the button for the elevator. "Nah. She's still in her probationary period. We don't need one."

"Gotcha," Matt said. "Now, can I go back to sleep?"

"Sure. Night, Matt."

Joe put his phone in his pocket as the elevator opened on the first floor. The hotel lobby was quiet as he passed through it on his way to the street. The desk clerk nodded, a smile curving his lips. Joe brought most of his dates to this place. It was discreet and classy and the women felt special when he took them there. It was also far from his home, where Ellie waited to nag him about where he was and who he was with.

She might believe what he told her in the end, but that didn't mean she didn't get hysterical from time to time. He tried, but couldn't drive that trait out of her. Can't fight nature, he supposed.

The street was empty as he exited the building. The doorman must have gone on break, because no one greeted him on his way out. Joe sighed. He'd have to get a cab.

He stepped onto the curb, craned his neck to

see up the street. Nothing. Joe took his phone out again and scrolled. Fuck, he never saved the number for the cab company. He typed the first few letters of the firm's car service into the phone when he heard a horn honk.

"Hey, boss," he heard Sherry whisper.

Joe glanced up in time to see headlights speeding toward him.

—

In the darkness, he heard sounds, felt pain, but it was separate from him. Other. Something tugged at his groin. Sometimes it was gentle, but more often it was too hard, too tight. Still, it didn't feel like his discomfort. His body, but someone else's skin.

He decided he must be drowning. The darkness was too thick, too substantive to be regular unconsciousness. It trapped him, held him down, so he couldn't rise. It stole his breath, forced something else into his lungs in its place, and just when it seemed he might succumb to its torture, it lifted, swirled around him, and allowed him to breath again.

He drifted along, listening and feeling, while trying to find a way to the surface. Time flipped on itself, turned, twisted and rolled, until he no longer recognized it. Drifting, drifting, until, finally, he saw light.

"Doctor," a hushed voice said. "He's waking up."

"Tighten the restraints," a woman said.

Restraints?

"He's going to be a problem."

A problem? Suddenly, it all came rushing back. Leaving the hotel. The truck.

Joe opened his eyes. A fresh-faced young man in dark pink scrubs fastened a leather restraint around his right wrist. A nurse? His eyes met Joe's and the fear Joe saw in those brown depths made him want to go back to sleep. Instead, he pulled on his confidence and forced it to wake up as well. "Where am I?"

The nurse tightened the strap on his left wrist. "Hospital."

"What happened?"

"You were hit by a truck," the woman said. Joe still couldn't see her. "You've been asleep for a long time."

"How long?"

"I have other patients," the woman said. "Get his sample and finish your rounds."

The nurse fussed with Joe's blankets, nervously glancing at the door before turning his attention back to Joe. "You've been in a coma for seven years. A lot's changed since your accident."

Seven years? Joe glanced around the room. It was dark. Too dark. The walls had been painted brown. Strange choice for a hospital room. Along the left side, he saw windows, but they'd been covered by black film. He could see out, sort of, but he suspected no one could see in.

Something tugged on his groin again. He looked down. While the blanket covered much of his body, he could see enough to know the nurse had attached a tube to his penis. It was attached to a canister that whirred as the nurse flipped a switch on the side.

"What are you doing?"

The nurse said nothing as he attached electrodes to Joe's balls and then pressed the base of the machine. A pulse emanated from the electrodes, causing his dick to harden.

"Wha—stop!"

He paid no attention to Joe's protests. He held the canister, eyes staring blindly at a spot on the wall across the room. Joe struggled, but the tube remained firmly attached to the end of his penis, the electronic pulses continued until, unable to fight it anymore, he climaxed.

As he twitched and grunted through the orgasm, the nurse held the canister, waiting several seconds after Joe's last spasm before removing the tube and the electrodes. He held up the canister. Joe's semen pooled at the bottom.

"Your samples are always plentiful. That's twice as much as I ever produce, even when I abstain for a long time."

"What the fuck are you doing?" Joe asked. "You can't just take that without my consent. Why am I restrained? I need to speak to someone in charge. This is a violation of my rights."

The nurse glanced at the door again, his fear almost palpable. "You have no rights."

"What?"

"I'll be back later."

"Nurse," a woman called from the doorway. "No talking."

He nodded, took the canister and hurried to the door.

"Hey!" Joe yelled. "You can't leave me here!"

But he did. Joe screamed for what felt like hours. A woman came in the room at some point, scowling at him, but silent. She pushed a needle into his arm, waited for him to settle, and then left. As sleep claimed him, Joe told himself it was a nightmare. He'd wake up and everything would be normal.

—

When Joe opened his eyes, the nurse sat in the chair next to his bed. He stood immediately, put his finger to his lips and then checked Joe's pulse. "Don't say anything," he whispered. "If they hear me talking to you, I'll be transferred to the banks."

"If who hears?"

The nurse looked at the door and then back to Joe. "My name is Two-oh-five. According to your arm, you're Thirty-fourteen."

Joe didn't look at his arm. "My name is Joe. What kind of name is Two-oh-five?"

"All men get numbers. We're not worthy of names."

"Okay, this is stupid. Untie these things. I'm leaving."

"I can't. It'd be certain death if I helped you."

Joe saw real fear in 205's eyes as he pretended to check Joe's IV line.

"Let's say I believe this," Joe said. "When did everything change?"

"About a year after your accident," he said. "They rose up."

"Who?"

"The women."

Joe scowled. He had to be joking.

"Organized one of those marches all over the world and then, while we were busy either kissing their ass or making fun of their little movement, they killed every single man in government."

"Impossible. You think I'm an idiot?"

"She organized it. It's why they put her in charge."

"Who?"

"We don't speak her name. It's not allowed."

Joe snorted. "Okay, enough with the bullshit. Your joke on coma guy didn't work."

"I wish I was joking."

"If we have no rights, why are you allowed to work here?"

"It's what I'm proficient at. I was just a kid at the time, so I got off easy. They sent me to a re-education camp. All of the male children had to go so they could determine who could adjust and who had to be eliminated."

"Re-what?"

"We're indoctrinated as disciples if we're successful. We work for them and they treat us kindly."

"This is insane."

"It sometimes seems like we are more like...possessions. Things they own and can do whatever they please with. I guess it's better than going to the banks." 205 shuddered.

"Banks?"

"Sperm banks," he said. "If you're no good for work or the banks, you're sent to the Coliseum. Sometimes, if she finds you pretty enough, she'll put you to work, even if you're uncooperative, but she's only done that twice. Those men probably wish they were dead."

"What Coliseum?

"It's just an arena, but we're supposed to call it a Coliseum. She says it sends a message to both men and women. Shows everyone how the New World Order works, so none of us is mistaken about our place."

"Yeah, still not buying it."

A muffled voice outside made 205 jumped away from Joe's bed. "I have to go."

Without another word, he scurried out of the room, head down. Joe stared at the empty space where he stood only seconds before. If the women rose up, why didn't the men just fight back? They were women, after all. How fucking hard could it be to put them in *their* place?

"Oh good," a woman said. "You're awake."

Joe watched as a thirty-something redhead entered the room. She wore a black pantsuit, crisp white blouse open at the collar, and sensible black shoes. As she rounded the bed, he admired her ass, high and firm, and her moderately sized tits.

Before the accident, he'd have chased a body like that. Maybe once he felt a little more like himself, he'd give her a go.

"My name is Sarah, but you will call me Mistress."

He laughed. "Sure."

"You're unfamiliar with the status quo, I imagine, as you've been unconscious since before the uprising."

"So, we're still going with this story?"

She lifted the blanket. "As an empty vessel, so to speak, you were invaluable to the breeding program, but she's immovable about your fate now that you're awake, I'm afraid."

"Who is?"

"You'll see." She retrieved the canister and electrode from the table near the wall. Joe's balls tightened at the sight of it. "I know. So impersonal. If you'd like to breed directly, rather than do it the sterile way, she's granted permission for...oh darn, I can't recall her name. She's next in line anyway."

"What are you talking about?"

"Some women prefer a surrogate, because pregnancy isn't a joy for all of us, although you fellas never seemed to get that fact." Sarah chuckled. "I for one hated the whole process, so the test tube thing was definitely a god-send for me.

No uterus or throbbing member required. Science is fantastic, isn't it?"

She lifted the blanket. Joe watched as she caressed his limp penis with one hand and cupped his balls with the other.

"There are some of us, though," she said, "who need the bonding experience of carrying our children in our bellies, so she allows us the choice of invitro, which eliminates the need or a male presence, or in person copulation, which allows the woman to have an actual male-female interaction, in which the child is conceived the old-fashioned way. Of course, the woman is given the male partner of her choice."

"What if the guy isn't interested?"

She smiled as she squeezed his balls. "They're always interested. The alternative is far too unpleasant for them not to be. You're quite virile, Thirty-fourteen. Already, your sperm dominates the bank. Women quite like your genetic profile, now that we've figure out a way to remove undesirable traits. Without the psychotic, narcissistic components, your offspring will be healthy, strong, and intelligent, not to mention extremely attractive. Always a bonus if you're given the task of conceiving male children. Makes it easier to love them when they're pretty."

"I see." He winced as she moved her hand over his dick in a rough, hurried fashion. "What are you doing?"

"Helping you get an erection. When she enters the room, you must look away. It's the law."

"Pardon?"

"You will not look her in the eye unless she grants permission."

"And if I do?"

She sighed, pausing in her aggressive attempt to jerk him off. "I suppose there is no punishment, as your fate is already decided. I will have to sedate you."

"If you put me to sleep, I won't get hard."

She laughed. "Who told you that?"

—

Joe woke again in darkness. He was seated now, but his arm tingled. He looked around. Wherever he was smelled like piss. He sat on something cold and hard, and his back pressed against something rough, like stone.

"Hello?" he called.

He tried to move his arm, but realized he'd been shackled, arms over his head.

"Hey!" he yelled. "A little help here?"

"Shh," a voice whispered in the dark. "They'll kill you quicker if you don't cause trouble."

"What?"

"Just shut it, hear? Sometimes she shows mercy, if you behave."

"Mercy?"

"Yeah. Quick death or, in some cases, a full pardon. You get to go to the banks or even a re-education camp. Just be patient and it'll all work out as it should."

Joe had to be dreaming. This was all a nightmare. He'd wake up and Ellie would be there, thankful he was alive. He'd go back to work, return to his place at the top, and he'd forget the torment his psyche seemed hell bent on inflicting upon him.

Somewhere beyond the walls of his prison, he heard cheering. "What's that?"

"It's starting," the voice said. "Quiet or the guard will make you wish you were dead."

The sound of metal clanking, the creak of rusted hinges, and hands under his arms. Joe fought as they uncuffed his wrists, but a cold, hard band of metal was strapped around his neck and his captors dragged him, like a dog, down a long hallway. He pulled, they pulled back, nearly snapping his neck in the process. He coughed, gagged, stumbled, but they paid no attention. Just kept dragging him along.

49

Finally, he saw a sliver of daylight. They walked through a door, and onto a field. He recognized the stadium. Often took clients there to woo them over a bit of baseball and beer. His captors, two women in black suits and sensible shoes, dragged him toward a podium. On it stood more women. They all wore masks. As they turned, his skin tightened. Each wore the leering plastic replica of an American president.

This must be a dream.

The woman wearing the Donald Trump mask advanced, helping the other two drag him onto the podium. They walked him to a large post, to which they fastened a short chain extending from his collar. Nixon came forward, took his arm and secured it to a beam running overhead. Then came Bush Sr., who secured his other arm. Joe, convinced it had to be a dream, let them do what they wanted without a fight.

He stood, aware of the over-capacity crowd cheering, taunting, and a few, for some reason, spitting at him, but his focus found a new target. At the edge of the podium stood a woman he thought he should recognize. She was tall, slim, with tits that belonged in a fucking museum, they were so perfect. Hard to be sure with the Obama mask on, but she looked a lot like Sherry. He'd know those tits anywhere.

She turned, lifted a knife, and without a word, threw it at him. It stuck in his side, just above his hip. Joe screamed. She threw another knife. This one pierced his thigh, alarmingly close to his balls. For a dream, the pain was disturbingly real. The cheers of the crowd rose to a deafening crescendo as the woman removed her mask. At once, the women on the podium, the men chained to the base of the stands, and those cheering went silent and got down on one knee.

Joe stared, his mouth dry, his body trembling.

She turned, another knife in her hand, and smiled. "Hey, boss."

"Sherry..." he managed.

"Eloise?" she called. "I believe the honor should be yours."

A woman wearing a Reagan mask approached. As she neared him, he recognized her eyes instantly.

"Ellie?" he said. "Don't do this. Please. You love me, Ellie. Remember all I've done for you."

Ellie unbuttoned the neck of her blouse, pulled the white fabric to the side, and showed him the scar on her throat; the one he'd given her soon after they got married. A joke, really. He only meant to scare her, but she struggled. "This is what you did for me, Joe. And this," she lifted the mask and pointed to her nose, slightly crooked from the time she pissed him off to the point of no return. He'd apologized. What man intended to ruin a pretty face that way? If she wasn't so fucking stupid—Ellie drove the knife into his belly and dragged it downward.

The crowd roared.

Joe panted, each breath becoming more agonizing than the last, as Ellie pushed the knife in again at the base of the first cut and then dragged it from one side of his belly to the other. Something heavy pushed down on his pelvis, and then he watched as Ellie and Sherry pulled his intestines out for all to see.

The crowd was electrified, their cheers so loud, so joyous, it drowned out everything, even his pain.

Dreaming. Had to be.

He closed his eyes as Ellie gave the knife to Sherry. Heat exploded in his groin and another deafening roar erupted from the crowd as the world slipped away.

—

In the darkness, he heard sounds, felt pain, but it was separate from him. Other. Something tugged at his groin. Sometimes it was gentle, but more often it was too hard, too tight. Still, it didn't feel like his discomfort.

He decided he must be drowning. The darkness was too thick, too substantive to be regular unconsciousness. It trapped him, held him down, so he couldn't rise. It stole his breath, forced something else into his lungs in its place, and just when it seemed he might succumb to its torture, it lifted, swirled around him, and allowed him to breathe again.

He drifted along, listening and feeling, while trying to find a way to the surface. Time flipped on itself, turned, twisted, and rolled, until he no longer recognized it. Drifting, drifting, until, finally, he saw light.

"Doctor," a hushed voice said. "He's waking up."

"Tighten the restraints," a woman said.

Restraints?

"He'll be a problem."

Suddenly, it all came rushing back. Leaving the hotel. The truck. Even this part, the woman, the restraints, felt familiar. Like he'd done this before.

Joe opened his eyes. A fresh-faced young man in dark pink scrubs fastened a leather restraint around his right wrist. A nurse? His eyes met Joe's and the fear Joe saw in those brown depths made him want to go back to sleep.

"Where am I?"

The nurse tightened the strap on his left wrist. "Hospital."

"Do I know you?"

The nurse smiled. "No."

"You were hit by a truck," the woman said. Joe still couldn't see her. "You've been asleep for a long time."

"How long?"

"I have other patients," the woman said. "Get his sample and finish your rounds."

The nurse fussed with Joe's blankets, nervously glancing at the door before turning his attention back to Joe. "You've been in a coma for seven years. A lot's changed since you got hit by that truck."

Right. Seven years. He knew that somehow.

Something tugged on his groin. He looked down. While the blanket covered much of his body, he could see enough to know the nurse had attached a tube to his penis. It was attached to a canister that whirred as the nurse flipped a switch on the side.

"What are you doing?"

He said nothing as he attached electrodes to Joe's balls and then pressed the base of the machine. A pulse coursed through his balls, causing his dick to harden almost instantly. "Wha—stop!"

He paid no attention to Joe's protests. He held the canister, eyes staring blindly at a spot on the wall across the room. Joe struggled, but the tube remained firmly attached to the end of his penis, the electronic pulses continued until, unable to fight it anymore, he climaxed.

As he twitched and grunted through the orgasm, the orderly held the canister, waiting several seconds after Joe's last spasm before removing the tube and the electrodes. He held up the canister. Joe's semen pooled at the bottom.

Joe didn't hear what he said next. Something about a bank and his sperm. The whole experience felt familiar, but so wrong.

"What the fuck are you doing?" Joe asked. "You can't just take that without my consent. Why am I restrained? I need to speak to someone in charge. This is a violation of my rights."

The nurse glanced at the door again, his fear almost palpable. "You have no rights."

"What?"

"You'll see."

"Nurse," a woman called from the doorway. "No talking."

He nodded, took the canister and hurried to

the door.

"Hey!" Joe yelled. "You can't leave me here!"

But he did. Joe screamed for help. A woman came in the room at some point, scowling at him, but silent. She pushed a needle into his arm, waited for him to settle, and then left. As sleep claimed him, Joe told himself it was a nightmare. That's why it seemed like he'd done it all before.

He'd wake up and everything would be normal.

—

Joe woke on a bed again, but this time he was in a small cell, his arms and legs still restrained, but with no blankets and no clothes. On his dick, someone had attached another pump. A machine beeped softly on his right side.

He looked at the door, which had a single narrow window. A woman's face stared back.

He knew her. How did he know her? Joe searched his memory. The pump started whirring, sucking mercilessly on his penis, forcing all other thoughts from his mind. He groaned, struggled against the leather straps holding his arms over his head, and tried to jerk the damn thing off his body.

A shock slithered up his balls. Joe gasped.

"Someone," he yelled, "please help!"

The door opened. A woman entered. Behind her, two others walked, heads down, clipboards raised. The lead moved to the bed, adjusted the electrodes sending sparks of agonizing pleasure through Joe's body, and then turned toward her companions.

"He won't do for in-person copulation. Too hysterical."

"Sedate him?"

She shrugged. "We'll see. I'm sure whoever chooses such a method of conception would want a partner able to perform, but you never know."

The women scribbled on their clipboards.

Joe struggled. "Hey! You can't do this. It's against every human right—"

"Human rights?" the woman asked. "You're...subhuman, at best."

He recognized that voice. Had heard it day in and day out for weeks. "Sherry?"

She leaned over the bed, brushed a piece of hair from his forehead and then smiled. "Hey, boss."

"This is illegal. They'll lock you up for life for kidnapping. You know that, right? Even you're not so stupid as to—"

"Take what I want from you without your consent?" she finished. "I warned you not to let the darkness in, but here we are. Funny thing, Joe, is that now I can take what I want, just as you did."

"What are you talking about?"

"You thought you could just harass me, terrorize me, rape me, and then fire me like I was nothing? Every action has a consequence."

"I never raped you. You wanted it."

She scowled.

"You did!" he insisted. "You didn't even try to fight back."

Both of her companions sighed.

Sherry opened the drawer of the small table next to his bed. She removed a scalpel. "I knew he'd be impossible."

"Yes," the other women said. "You said so."

"Let's just be done with him, shall we?"

They nodded. Joe didn't feel the scalpel go in, but he felt the warmth of his blood pooling on his neck and behind his head before it filled his lungs.

—

When Joe opened his eyes, the nurse sat in the chair next to his bed. He stood immediately, put his finger to his lips and then checked Joe's pulse. "Don't say anything," he whispered. "She will know."

"Who will know?"

The nurse looked at the door and then back to Joe. "My name is Two-oh-five. According to your arm, you're Thirty-fourteen."

Joe looked at his arm. Along the wrist, someone had written the numbers 3-0-1-4 in black marker...or was that a tattoo? "My name is Joe."

"Men don't have names, Thirty-fourteen."

"Well I fucking do," Joe said. He remembered this guy. Remembered this conversation. Christ, what was happening?

"All men get numbers," the nurse said. "We're not worthy of names."

"Okay, this is stupid. Untie these things. I'm leaving."

"It'd be certain death if I helped you."

Joe saw real fear in 205's eyes as he pretended to check Joe's IV line. "Next you're going to talk about an uprising. We already did this."

"About a year after your accident," 205 said. "They rose up, yes, but we haven't had this conversation, because you've been in a coma for seven years."

"The women rose up?"

"Yes."

Joe scowled. He had this conversation and died at the end. Had to be a dream. "I know," he said. "They organized one of those marches all over the world and then killed every single man in government."

"How did you know?"

"I told you, we've discussed this before."

"But we haven't. Perhaps you overheard while you were asleep. Yes, that's logical."

Joe snorted. "Okay, enough with the bullshit. Your joke on coma guy didn't work."

A muffled voice outside made 205 jump away from Joe's bed. "I have to go."

Without another word, the nurse scurried out of the room, head down. Joe stared at the empty space where he stood only seconds before. 205 might be too afraid, but Joe wasn't. He'd put these bitches back in their place as soon as he got out of the restraints.

"Oh good," a woman said. "You're awake."

Joe watched as a thirty-something redhead entered the room. She wore a black suit, sans tie, and sensible black shoes. He remembered her too. Nice ass, average tits. Sarah, she'd said.

"My name is Sarah, but you will call me Mistress."

He laughed. "Okay."

"You're unfamiliar with the status quo, I imagine, as you've been unconscious since before the uprising."

"So, we're still going with this story?"

She lifted the blanket. "As an *empty vessel*, so to speak, you've been invaluable to the breeding program, but she's immovable about your fate now that you're awake, I'm afraid."

"I know. She's going to execute me in the Coliseum."

"Who told you?"

"No one. I'm in a fucking nightmare that won't end."

She smiled. "It's been requested that you be part of an in-person copulation, but you must promise to be on your best behavior."

"Sure."

"You will not look her in the eye, nor will you do anything until she tells you to do it. Understood?"

Maybe they'd take off the restraints. "Got it."

She eyed him warily. "Perhaps sedation is best..."

—

Joe woke in his office, at his desk. No, not his desk. He looked around, saw a desk next to him, the bank of elevators; he was at Sherry's desk.

He stood, straightened his pants, and leaned toward the man at the desk next to him. "Where's Sherry?"

The man didn't look up from his computer. "We don't use their first names, Thirty-fourteen. You know that."

Joe's chest twisted uncomfortably. Still not out of the damn dream. The elevator doors chimed. He looked up. Sherry emerged, a gaggle of men behind her. She had a phone to her ear, and barked orders while she walked.

"Sherry," he said. "What the hell—?"

"You'll address me as Mistress. Honestly, I don't know what's gotten into you. Lucky you're so pretty or I'd fire your ass and send you to the banks."

Joe frowned. "This is your desk. You're my assistant."

"Is that right?" Sherry smiled. "Eighteen-fifty-two, take Thirty-fourteen downstairs. He needs some air to clear his pretty head. When you're ready to work, Thirty-fourteen, you may come back upstairs."

Joe watched Sherry march to his door, enter his office, and disappear inside. The man she'd told to escort him touched Joe's elbow. He pulled away. "I know where outside is, asshole. Fuck off."

The asshole backed away. "Please, don't piss her off. She's a right..." he glanced around before lowering his voice, "bitch."

"I'll go on my own. Find a way to end this nightmare."

He left the office. On the elevator, he closed

his eyes, willing himself awake. It chimed, indicating the doors were open, and Joe exited into the lobby. As he walked toward the glass doors, he noticed the men walking outside were all dressed alike. Joe looked at his own clothes. He wore the same grey shirt and pants as the others. They walked with their heads down, eyes on the ground. Whatever was happening here, he'd stop it once and for all.

Joe left the building. The air was cold. A bitter wind blew against his face, but he didn't look down, although it'd be easier to breath if he did. He watched as women passed the men, heads held high, and now and then, they'd say something to the men or grab their ass, their crotch...clearly, he was feeling some misguided guilt over Sherry. Why else would he have these fucked up dreams?

A pair of women in police uniforms walked toward him. Joe ducked into an alley. Had to be the most vivid dream he'd ever experienced. The coldness of the wind, the way the piss smell permeating the alley seemed to fill his mouth as well as his sinuses, and the dull ache in his head; all felt so real. So present.

"Hey," a woman called from the end of the alley. "You're not supposed to be out alone."

Joe turned. The woman was easily six feet tall.

Sturdily built too. Christ, her arms were bigger than his thighs, and Joe prided himself on his muscular physique. "Fuck off," he muttered, backing toward the opposite end of the alley.

She laughed. "Only an idiot would dare to speak to a woman that way," she said. "Let me re-educate you, sweetheart."

Joe continued to back away. She reached behind her as she closed the distance between them. Before he could make sense out of what was happening, she lunged, grabbed the front of his shirt, and slammed him against the brick wall. The cold stone bit into his shoulder blades. He struggled, but she put the business end of a gun under his chin.

"You be a good boy," she said, "and I'll make this quick."

She groped his crotch, then squeezed his balls way too hard while kissing his neck just beneath his ear. "Mistress must've been hiding you somewhere," she whispered. "I'd have remembered your sweet ass." She cupped his ass cheek as she spoke.

Joe wanted to climb out of his skin. He wanted to run. To fight. The gun, though, made that difficult. If not for the weapon, he'd have kicked her ass.

Wait...

She continued her assault, releasing the drawstring at the top of his pants and then pushing her cold hands inside. Joe gagged on the vomit that burned his throat. He pushed, she pushed back harder, yanking his dick with such force he thought he might pass out.

He stopped fighting. Let her do what she wanted.

"That's right, honey," she whispered, "just let it happen."

As he submitted, she eased off him a bit. Joe used her arrogance—imagine believing *she* could overpower *him*—against her. He waited until the pressure of the gun barrel eased and then kicked her hard, grabbing the gun as she jumped away.

One shot. She crumpled to the ground. He heard shouts at the end of the alley.

"Stop!" a woman yelled.

Joe backed away as the police officers advanced down the alley toward him.

"Put down your weapon!" one said.

Joe knew already the other end of the alley held a dumpster and a fence. He could try to escape, but he'd never climb the fence before they shot him down.

Suddenly, he remembered how the other

dreams ended. Every time, every single time, he died and it was over.

He faced the women running toward him. Three more had joined the officers in their pursuit. Joe put the gun under his chin. This should wake him up.

—

Joe woke in a hospital. The pain in his face was indescribable. Machines beeped somewhere nearby, and a too-bright light shone in his eyes.

Not like before. Was he truly awake now? He swallowed, but his throat felt tight. Hot.

"Water," he tried to say, but his voice was barely more than a whisper.

"Joe?" Ellie said. Hands on his arm. "Nurse! I think he's awake."

More hands. Whispering. A package rustling. Something tingly in his fingers. Then the pain in his face faded. Someone put something to his lips. A straw. Joe tried to pull the water into his mouth, but he only managed a few drops. The rest rolled over his chin and onto his chest.

"It's okay, baby," Ellie said. "The doctor told us it'd take time to relearn a few things. How are you feeling?"

"Happened?" he managed to whisper.

She stroked his hand. "They found you in an

alley, sweetheart. It looked like you tried to kill yourself."

No. That wasn't real. Joe lifted his hand. No restraints. He touched his head. Bandages.

"Shame," he heard another voice. Familiar, but he couldn't place it. "That handsome face ruined..."

"Sherry," Ellie whispered, "he's more than just a pretty face. Besides, he's got me to take care of him. I love him no matter what."

How did Ellie know Sherry?

"Good morning," a man's voice said. "How's the patient today?"

Joe listened as Ellie told the doctor he was awake.

"Good thing you followed him," Ellie was saying. "We might have lost him."

"He just seemed off," Sherry said. "I was worried."

Sherry hadn't followed him. A truck hit him. Joe opened his mouth, but nothing came out.

"Don't try to talk," the doctor said. "Your vocal chords need time to heal, as does the rest of your—the rest of you. In time, you may regain feeling in your legs, but we'll count each blessing as it comes instead of focusing too much on that."

Joe realized he couldn't feel anything beneath his waist. "No. This isn't real. Still dreaming"

He just had to wake up and everything would be okay. Joe pulled at the bandages on his head. The doctor barked orders. Joe tried to sit up, tried to wake himself up. Nothing worked.

Hands held him down. Sherry and Ellie talked over the doctors, urging him to settle. Finally, he was too tired to continue. Someone pulled a blanket over his shoulders. He let them fuss over him. Ellie kissed his cheek. "Be back soon," she whispered. He felt the cool air replace her presence, and then another hand on his chest. Sherry's hair tickled his chin as she leaned close, kissed his bandaged forehead and adjusted his blanket.

"Next time you're alone with a woman," she whispered, "maybe you'll show a little respect." She stroked his chest and then his stomach. He felt a slight pressure near his hip, but then it disappeared. "Oh dear," she said. "I guess there might not be a next time."

Tears warmed his cheeks, soaking the bandages around his chin. "I'll kill you, bitch."

She sighed. "You let the dark inside you, Joe, so you have no one to blame for this but yourself. I hoped you'd get what you deserved. Actually, for a long time, I prayed someone would kill *you*. This is better, though. More...appropriate, considering the way you behaved." She stood, opened the curtains, and then picked up a mirror from the table next to his bed. Smiling, she lifted it high enough for him to see his reflection. "Who's going to fuck you now with a face like that?"

¤

"You think that's funny? Woman ain't taking over anything. How much longer 'til we get to the shop or whatever?" Tobias said, sullen, no longer looking out his window, instead staring hard at the big orange head atop the big shoulders that sat behind the big steering wheel.

Eleonore still had her phone to her ear. She'd redialled Ross more than a dozen times and wasn't about to give up, but for some reason, the story made her feel a little better. As if there might be some kind of justice in the universe.

"Plain stupid," Tobias said, the words a grumble. "You know what, what's your name? I'm going to talk to your boss."

The driver ignored this, really digging into the thick threads at the edge of his scalp. Eleonore watched this intently, but spoke to Tobias, "You know, it's like you're two people sometimes."

The driver let his hand fall from his head and pointed out the window. "The man who lived in that house had something like that."

Tobias tutted and Eleonore redialled her son's cellphone.

"Something just like that," the driver said.

# MY LOVE, DO NOT WAKE

## Philip Fracassi

I fell in love with Martin during the hottest week of the year; of the last decade, some said, and no one in their right mind would argue. Henry, my husband, was working that summer in a downtown depository where the only air-conditioning involved industrial fans that rattled at high speeds and the natural airflow sweeping through the large delivery bay door they kept open during the summer. Only a warped accordion gate separated the inventory—copy paper, that is, miles and miles of it—from the riff-raff who shuffled and scuttled through the streets and alleyways of downtown Los Angeles' warehouse district. Most days he'd be sweat-soaked by noon, arriving home at six-thirty (or seven-thirty if he went for a beer with those men he worked with) as sticky and miserable as a toddler locked alone in a hot car while some idiot mother shopped at the supermarket (likely buying liquor and cigarettes).

I met my sweet love on a Saturday. The Friday evening prior, Henry had come home ripe with that lascivious *parfum du jour* of the working class, a mixture of body odor and cheap beer (which he seemingly splashed on daily), and announced he was going to Sam's Barbershop the next morning to have the barber (a fat, greasy man with a disgusting moustache; and yes, his name really was Sam. How quaint, right?) quote—shave my whole damn head clean—unquote.

I told him it was a splendid idea and I meant it. His hair was too long anyway, tangled black curls that sprang over his ears like broken coils, crossed his forehead in a raven's wing swoop and floated across the back of his neck like rolled hay—and probably just as itchy, especially in the heat. When it dampened, which was every day this particular summer, the black mop stuck to his forehead and cheeks, dripped sweat into his eyes, and likely kept his body temperature ten degrees higher than it needed to be, the head being the primary area where heat and bad thoughts escape.

Oh my...I'm sorry...but all this talk of Henry's overheated head has got me blushing. But we'll get to that.

True to his word, Henry awoke early the next morning, made a pot of coffee—too strong, as always—and kissed me on the cheek as he brushed past me out the door. "Gonna get a shave while I'm at it! Clean up nice for my beautiful wife," he said, and I offered a smile which became a grimace when the door shut behind him.

I ran my own assortment of errands—flower shop (I adored fresh flowers in the house at all times), stationery store for new paper and a set of good writing pens, a boutique dress shop where I loved to browse but couldn't afford a stitch much less an entire dress, and then a pop-in to the grocer's for the makings of whatever meal Henry would all but swallow whole that evening. When I was younger and more impressionable (more in *love)*, I would have added a six-pack of cold beer, or a bottle of good gin and a quart of tonic, to the list for my darling husband. After a few years of marriage, however, watching him guzzle his beer and slop down his gin-and-tonics become tedious—at first, a bore; later, a labor.

Pork chops, scalloped potatoes, green beans,

and water would have to do. I preferred wine, myself, but rarely bought any for the house. I wouldn't want to accidentally class the place up. But no beer for Henry, at least not from *moi*. If anyone needed a drink around this house, it was me.

But let's talk about that night.

When I first saw him post haircut, I have to admit it was startling. He was lounging on the couch like a tired tiger, smiling at me as I walked through the door, and I felt a momentary prick of joy (and okay, lust)—such a rarity I mistook it for a dizzy spell at first. He looked *good*. He looked young and virile with his bristle-black head and his clean-shaven cheeks and jaw. His eyes sparkled and it reminded me—maybe not of why I fell in love with him—generally, of *love* itself. It may as well have been a childhood locket sprawled there on the sofa, the miniature photos within that of a childhood crush, or a pet I'd loved unconditionally. Like a cat. Or a dog.

"Don't you clean up well," I said, an actor in the world's most boring play, spoken for an audience of one.

He sprang from the sofa and grabbed the grocery bag from my arms, kissed me on the lips. "I feel like a new man!" he hollered as he walked away, all skinny ass and knuckles.

I think that was the first moment I noticed the odd bulges on the back of his skull.

I became distracted, however, when he began grousing about my not having bought him beer (this is the part when I flash the audience an eye-roll and a shake of the head, as in: *Can you believe this shit? Kill me now, will you?*).

After pork chops, some television (him) and a *New Yorker* article on contemporary political literature (me), it was time for bed: seven minutes of missionary position and then off to dreamland for our head-sheared hero and his bored, dutiful wife.

That night I couldn't sleep. My mind buzzed like angry bees: all hard thoughts and splintered emotions. I felt like I was dancing on an eggshell in high heels. Stilettos.

I am in my late-thirties (I'm sure it's a shock to men everywhere that even women feel a certain crisis when it comes to the approach of middle-age), and I lay there feeling sorry for myself, miserable and cotton-headed. Like a once pretty doll that had gone out of fashion, left lying awkwardly and forgotten in a child's bedroom no longer occupied, the resident having grown up and moved on to wonderful things, thrilling adventures and breathtaking romance, leaving the dumb fucking doll behind to stare, glassy-eyed, at the ceiling.

It was pathetic, sure, but so many things are it can hardly count as noteworthy.

I must have eventually fallen asleep, because the first time I heard Martin whispering in my ear I thought it was a dream—a sweet dream: I was in an endless field, a beast of land with a broad back of blooming cotton, the pure white bursting like fur from pods as far as the eye could see. A green-leaf horizon and a sky of azure blue so brilliant and vast that it didn't seem like sky at all, but space itself. In my mind the universe wasn't filled with cold black nothingness and candy-colored galaxies, orbiting planets and exploding stars, vacuous black holes; it was *blue*. All of it. And it went on forever.

*Olivia...*

The voice of God? Ultimately not; simply the sound of an unseen lover—both far away and so intimately close it gave me goosebumps—in the dream world and, I suspect, in the real world as well.

*Olivia...*

In the dream I spin to look at the man whispering in my ear—and keep spinning. The crops of cotton blurred and the sky tilted and then my eyes shot open. I gasped at the revelation of the dark, the stillness and despair of my bed, and the night surrounding it.

"Olivia…"

His voice—not in the dream but *here*, in my bed—came again, so close I felt I could reach out and touch it. I gave my head a little shake, the pillowcase wet beneath my sweat-clumped hair, my cheeks moist with the night's heat. I stayed still a moment, let my brain catch up to things—realign, as it were, with reality.

What was this voice? Was I imagining it? If not…

Suddenly I was afraid. Was someone in the room with Henry and me? It was ridiculous, of course. A burglar? A rapist? A murderer who happened to know my name? It made no sense. I licked my lips and reached a hand toward my husband's bare shoulder, his back to me as it always was while he slept.

His bristly head was buried in shadow, which is why I didn't see Martin.

Not at first.

"Olivia…"

The voice was a whisper, harsh and injured. Sad. Desperate.

It came from Henry…*or did it?*

I shifted my body closer to my husband, focused on the hair carpeting the back of his head. Something along the surface of his short-shaven head was *moving*. And when it moved, that voice came once more.

"Olivia, please..."

And then I could see it.

See *him*.

What moved on the back of Henry's head, just above the point where the skull bulges away from the neck, was a mouth. A slim, pretty mouth with thin red lips sprung with fine hairs like the moustache of a prepubescent boy. Even in that moment, despite the admitted strangeness of it, I badly wanted to kiss those lips, to feel the gentle wisp of those fine moist hairs against my tongue.

Entranced, I put a trembling hand on Henry's shoulder, and slowly *pushed*—gently, so he wouldn't wake, but with enough pressure to move him into a pool of pale moonlight coming through the bedroom window and the thin lace curtains which covered it—revealing the detail of Henry's head, the mouth I now realized was speaking to me.

Was *calling* to me.

Henry groaned a little and sunk his face deeper into the pillow, the back of his head now fully caught in the silver light.

I gasped—not in fear, but in *wonder*.

Above the mouth, also slightly obscured by those fine, cropped hairs, was a wide, flat nose. It was no more than a bug bite in height on Henry's scalp, and the little nostrils were squeezed and horizontal, slits instead of holes. Above this fine nose were two milky eyes, half-lidded. The eyeballs were the only part of Henry's head not covered in bristled hair, although the eyelids were; so that when he blinked—Martin, I mean—those glorious blind eyes vanished, as if they had never been.

I didn't think he could see me, or see at all, given the colorless vacancy of the glistening white pools beneath the lids, but they were stunning nonetheless. When they caught the moonlight they appeared as pools of mercury, and it made me think of how an angel's eyes might appear. Or a god's. They seemed infinite.

The lips parted and, in the better light, I could see the black cavern of a mouth behind them, burrowing back toward Henry's brain stem. Inside were two rows of tiny white teeth.

In that moment I wanted nothing more than to slip my fingers inside that mouth, feel its warmth; I shivered in lust at the thought of those nubby teeth clenching down on my slim knuckles. I purred like a cat and felt my body heat rise. I moved closer, put my hands gently on either side of my husband's head, and looked deeply into this new face. This stranger in my bed.

"I'm here," I said quietly, barely a whisper as I was deeply afraid of waking Henry, of having him spoil this moment, this newfound bit of magic in my life. "Can you...hear me?"

A smile creased the tough skin of Henry's scalp. "Oh, yes, I can...I can smell you now, as well... I wish I could see, but..." Those mercurial eyes seemed to shift back and forth, then widened and settled once more on emptiness, thwarted. "Perhaps one day."

"What...I mean...*who* are you?" I asked, unconsciously stroking behind Henry's ear; what I thought of as a temple, or a cheekbone.

"My name is Martin," he said in a gentle, raspy voice, like the bustle of dry leaves on a windblown fall day. "I've wanted this for so long, Olivia. I could never...but, now, I *can*. I've wanted to see you, to be with you."

I stared into his eyes, at those warm fuzz-covered lips, the cute flare of nostrils. It was unreal and amazing, but my silence must have worried him.

"I can go back," he said haltingly. "If I'm scaring

you, I can go back."

I kissed him. Gently, then with more heat. I kissed his lips, his eyelids, and his flat nose. Felt his breath. Henry groaned but neither one of us noticed, or cared.

"Please, stay with me," I said.

"All right," he replied, and it seemed to me, even in those first moments, that some of the milkiness of his eyes cleared away like blown clouds, and the nub of his nose grew outward a millimeter or two, like a swelling flower bud.

We continued to talk the whole night through, and when I finally fell asleep at his side, clutching Henry's body, I was thinking of it, already, as Martin.

After that first night, I longed, continuously, for the dark.

—

I woke to find the room filled with horrible sunlight, searing and intrusive. Henry was gone, and the curtains had been thrown open wide, his way of giving me hell for staying in bed while he went off to work, I suppose. He's nothing if not clever with his cruelties.

*Henry!*

I sat up with a shot, remembering the night and all its glory. Had it been a dream? Certainly not. Impossible! But now, in the shadowless bedroom, I wished I had woken when Henry was still home, to see if Martin was still there, still visible. I imagined those white eyes looking at me as Henry walked away, to the shower, and I shivered with desire.

I threw back the sheets and leapt from bed, began pacing the warm hardwood floor. I was a wreck! A teenage girl longing for her first crush! I bit my nails cruelly, shoved back the mangy curls of my hair so I could think, *THINK.*

Would Henry notice Martin? Was it even possible? Likely not, no. Of course, it was impossible to see the back of one's own head without a mirror...but even then. Difficult. Tricky, for sure. Angles are...

But he could feel it, right? Surely he...if he were to scratch at the back of his scalp, for example, wouldn't his nails dig into one of Martin's angelic eyes? Slip into a nostril, push between those fine lips? And then...what? He'd scream! He'd run to the nearest co-worker and ask for an inspection of his head, and then *that* man would scream and there would be doctors, surgeries... OH MARTIN OH GOD!

I ran to the hallway and leapt for the phone.

"The number? What is..." I dropped the phone

and hurried to the kitchen, grabbed the notepad we kept amidst a pile of clutter which served as a makeshift address book, and found the number to Henry's downtown warehouse. The kitchen's bay window faced the front lawn, the sidewalk and the street beyond, giving the outside world a clean shot of my naked body. I felt a moment of horror before realizing I didn't care, didn't give one iota if my bare ass was the mailman's happy morning surprise. Let him have it if it meant saving Martin's life.

I hustled back to the phone and dialed the number on the notepad, just beneath Henry's all-caps *mot juste*: WORK. Hard to fault his obviousness, especially as this was an...

"Hello?"

A burly voice, likely the chief of the stackers.

"Yes, hello," I said, all charm and sex. "This is Henry's wife, Liv. Is he available to speak? I just need a moment."

"Oh," the man said, "Oh, sure. Is everything okay?"

"Yes, yes, fine. Thank you. I...well, it's silly. I just need to ask him about something here at the house, something I'm trying to fix."

"Oh, sure," the burly voice said, and I imagined a fat-bellied man with coarse arm hair and a neck beard, scratching at his jaw while trying to piece together what I looked like, if I was good in bed. "I see," he said, sounding relieved at such an easy subject. *Fixing,* after all, was what men did. "Let me get Henry for you, Liv. Hold on a sec."

I paced as much as the phone cord would allow. Finally, Henry came on the line. Yes, he said, work was fine. Yes, yes, he felt okay. No, he didn't need the car and yes, I could take it anywhere I needed. What a silly question, he said. Are you okay, he said.

No mention of Martin. No screaming. I could almost imagine him on the phone, there in the warehouse, scratching and rubbing at the back of his head, the calming bristle of the sheared hair, the glorious absence of a second nose, mouth, white eyes.

I breathed a sigh of such relief that for a moment I loved that stupid man. Loved him for the heartening news he gave me while playing the role of blessed messenger, telling me everything was just fine, that horror had been averted, that life could go on.

When I hung up, I was so giddy I leapt under the sheets and spent ten more minutes in bed, with my hand, thinking of Martin.

After—feeling much less tense—I started a

shower and considered options for my day.

—

By the time Henry came home, I'd already prepared dinner—lasagna and salad with blue cheese, his favorite—bought the poor dear a bottle of the gin he loved so much, and stopped by the pharmacy to pick up the prescription of sleeping pills I'd asked my doctor for.

"Well well, look at this!" he exclaimed as he came into the kitchen, seeing the table set and the lasagna cooling on the stove. When I handed him an ice-cold gin and tonic with a slice of lime pressed onto the edge I thought his eyes would pop out of his head. "What's the occasion?" he said, slurping on the drink like I knew he would. I gritted my teeth with grace.

"It's hot, you've been working hard," I said, and ran my hands along the sides of his neck, up past his ears and let my fingers roam the back of his head. "I'm just glad... OH!"

I must have flushed because Henry looked concerned. He set his drink down and put his hands firmly on my arms, pulling my own hands down to my sides. I allowed this reluctantly, for you see, I was still swooning at the feel of Martin's tongue running itself between the crease of my fingers. Blood rushed to my hips and thighs and it was all I could do not to spin the brute around and put my mouth on Martin's, feel that sly tongue slide between my lips.

"Here, here, sit down, babe," Henry said. "Let me get you something."

"No, please, I'm fine," I said, allowing him to guide me to the dinner table. "Why don't you go wash up and we'll have dinner."

"You sure?" he said, looking hard at my face, probably trying to understand why my cheeks were bursting like roses.

"Yes, don't be silly," I replied, and gave him my best smile, the one he liked to call my see you later smile, because when he saw it he knew he'd, well, you know...be *getting some* that night. When we were first married, I'd flash the see you later over a nice restaurant dinner, or at the movies when our hands met, loving how much it excited him.

Now I used it like a weapon. A tool to manipulate—a promise I rarely ever followed-through on anymore. It still worked, though. Funny how stupid men are, isn't it?

As he walked away, down the hall toward the bathroom, I stared.

Martin watched me with a smile and a knowing glint in his eyes. He must have been some kind of magic to appear and disappear the way he did, and when I gave him a little wave, part of me wasn't at all surprised to see Henry's fingers shake a little *toodle-loo* right back at me.

So that's how it was, I thought, and stood to make my husband a plate of food and a fresh drink, understanding that Martin, miraculously, was beginning to take control.

—

Henry started to yawn as I cleared the dishes. I would imagine so. He'd had three drinks, the last two of which were handsomely spiked with crushed pills. I just hoped I hadn't overdone it.

I had no desire to drag him to the bedroom.

Throughout the meal he had talked and I laughed, pretending it was like old times. Slyly, I'd brought my vanity mirror from the bathroom and set it on the countertop behind him. It was delicious to steal glances at Martin while Henry yammered on about paper products and his desire to do more with his life, et cetera and so forth.

Martin's reflection smiled at me and I grinned back. Once, Henry caught me looking over his shoulder and turned his head. I almost burst out laughing at the poor brute. Even Martin appeared to be stifling laughter—and wouldn't that have been a situation!

"What are you looking at?" Henry said, half-smiling and already dopey from the drugs. Red sauce dabbled his chin and his eyes were glassy, his mouth stupid and slack.

"Just you, dear," I said truthfully. "Just you."

—

That night, while Henry snoozed heavily as a corpse, Martin and I made love for the first time.

Oh, I know what you're thinking, but trust me when I say that it worked out just fine. It was easy to turn Henry's head just *so*, and I made the inspired decision to lay a pillowcase over his face so I wouldn't be distracted from my lover's sidelong expressions of pleasure.

Afterword, I settled Henry face-down so Martin and I could talk privately. He was obviously well-educated, and when I inquired about his wealth of knowledge he told me that he had simply absorbed all the things Henry himself had lost.

"It's amazing the information the mind retains on a subconscious level," he said as I stroked the back of Henry's ears, gently kissed that fuzzy mouth. "Heck, I probably know more about Henry than Henry does," he said, and I felt myself cool at his words.

"Let's not talk about him, shall we? I'd rather not, anyway."

Martin looked concerned but didn't press. I

suppose he thought I was referring to a guilty conscious, and perhaps, to a small degree, I was. But it was more about *forgetting*. Forgetting that on the other side of this wonderful man was my onerous husband, stuck to my lover like a Siamese twin. It infuriated me, but I knew there was nothing to be done; so I tried my best to enjoy Martin for who he was, and what he was.

"I wish…" I said dreamily, and when he smiled I noticed his teeth seemed slightly larger, his tongue more plump, his lips more well-formed. And his eyes…

I pushed myself up on an elbow and stared.

Marble-sized irises floated in the white.

They were faint, but they were most certainly *there*. Further—as I tried my best to discern in the pale moonlight—I could have sworn they were the most lovely shade of brown, all but dissolved by the cloudy white of his blindness.

"Your eyes," I said.

"Yes," he replied, "I can almost make you out, now. You're a shadow still, all black and white, and the dark certainly doesn't help. But light is getting in, most certainly. Soon, perhaps, I'll be able to look upon you with my own eyes, not have to rely on the sight of…well…another."

I was beyond ecstatic and told him so. I kissed

him hungrily and when Henry started to snore, I straddled his behind and pushed his face harder into the pillow, hoping to shut him up so he would stop interrupting us with his pathetic existence. "I don't understand. Are you...what? Evolving?"

Martin nodded. "It seems so. I do feel stronger, more in control. I can taste things now. For instance, the shampoo...it's bitter on my tongue, something I've never experienced before."

"Oh my love, I shall buy the most wonderful, expensive, sweet-tasting shampoo I can find! How cruel of me to subject you to something so common."

"It's fine, Olivia, just fine," he said. "I only meant that, yes, I seem to be expanding my senses. Here, watch this."

And then the most glorious thing happened.

Henry's arms lifted and reached backward to grip each my bare thighs. The hands slid upward to my hips and held me there. I moaned in pleasure as he squeezed my flesh.

"I'm afraid that's as high as I'm able," he said breathily, obviously as excited as I was. "Maybe with some, you know, stretches, I could..."

I saw despair flicker on his face. I gripped his hands tightly in my own, bent down and smothered him with a long, sensuous kiss. "Do not worry, my love," I breathed into him. "I am yours and you are mine, that is all that matters."

"Until he wakes, you mean," Martin said, trying to sound glum, but I could tell I'd lifted his mood.

"Well," I said, the urge to make love again rushing through me like fire, my fingers already groping for the empty pillowcase, my husband's makeshift mask, "that is a puzzle we shall put together another night, *mon amour.*"

"Oui," he replied, laughing. "*Revenons à nos moutons.*"

"Baaaaa," I said, and kissed him.

—

A week later, I decided to tell Martin my plan. After all, there was only so much one could do with sleeping pills and carefully-set mirrors.

Ironically, Henry had never seemed more happy. I think, despite his being unconscious during my affair, some biological part of him must have been experiencing a taste of the emotions Martin himself felt. Love. Lust. That giddy joy of a blossoming relationship. The mind-bending sex. He was there, after all, for every moment of it— everything from the late-night conversations to the whispered promises to the bursting orgasms. In many ways, he was a participant.

I'd made my decision, however. It was time to cut Henry from the equation.

Martin, meanwhile, had blossomed beneath my tender care. His eyes were indeed brown, and by the third day of our *affaire de cœur* he saw me as plainly as I saw him. His nose had grown as well, and the first dark formations of eyebrows arched above his eyelids. His mouth was fuller, moved more easily, and when he laughed (only when Henry was properly sedated, of course), he looked just like any other man.

There were...problems, of course. Like any budding relationship, there were issues to address, wrinkles to iron flat.

Henry's hair growth, for one.

After a few days, Martin was becoming more obscured than I cared for, and kissing him became a bit too much like kissing, well, the back of someone's head, not to put too fine a point on it. I purchased electric shears from the beauty supply (along with organic shampoo and conditioner, imported from Paris, made from apples and oatmeal without a chemical in-between), and convinced Henry to let me keep his hair tight to the scalp. I almost suggested he let me shave him bald—the very idea of which brought such a flame to my libido that I gasped and grew faint—but concluded it was a bridge too far.

He acquiesced, but haltingly. Even a gorilla can sense danger and I think that, despite Henry's overall positive disposition, he was beginning to wonder about me just a tiny bit. Of course, if he feared I was cheating on him he'd have been only half-right, but it was of no consequence, regardless.

I didn't foresee Henry being in the picture much longer.

That night, eight blissful days after Martin first appeared to me, I revealed myself to *him* completely, put myself so far out on a limb that, had he rejected the idea, rejected *me* for even considering it, I may have easily slipped from that delicate branch of joy and not stopped falling until the ground came up to crush the life from me.

As I'd hoped, however, Martin held little objection.

"We must be careful," he said. "I don't fully know how this works." He lifted a hand and turned it this way and that, as if testing a theory. "When he's asleep, I can take control. Here...let me try something."

Awkwardly, Martin pulled aside the sheet. Awestruck, I watched as Henry's body turned and sat upright in the bed. Martin was still looking at me, but his face was full of concentration. I could tell he was trying to sort out the musculature of the operation. The bone structure, of course, was all wrong, but I was desperately intrigued by the performance.

Henry's legs went over the edge of the bed, and then he stood.

"See here," he said, and looked down at me. "I have an idea."

Slowly, his flesh silver in the moonlight, my husband *turned around,* and it was Henry's sleeping face I saw as he started to walk *backward.*

Like a robot being operated by remote control, he walked stiffly along the wall, feeling out to either side like a blind man which, in a way, I suppose he was. Henry, eyes closed and mouth curved into a frown, staggered to the foot of the bed, stumbling only once over a stray shoe he must have left on the floor. Martin cursed softly but didn't seem daunted in the slightest.

"Oh, Martin!" I gasped as he moved confidently across the bedroom floor. He turned and smiled wildly, stiffly lifting his elbow-locked arms toward me.

"Easy!" he exclaimed, clearly excited. "I mean, the skeleton is my enemy here, and small tasks will be difficult. Sitting down to a meal will have its

93

challenges, but all-in-all…"

I sprang off the bed and ran to him. This was beyond my wildest fantasies! *It could work!* I thought as I hugged him. *It could actually work!*

"But if, I mean, if we…*kill* him," I ventured, "are we sure…"

Martin nodded, deep in thought but not distraught. "I'm almost positive," he said. "If you're sure it's what you want…"

I screamed in joy and smothered the poor man in kisses. I crawled back onto the bed and watched him hungrily. "Go and get me a glass of water!" I yelled, exalted at the thrill of it. I felt like a mad scientist who had just brought her greatest creation to life. I swooned with power.

"All right!" he said, and laughed as he walked backward out the door and toward the kitchen, Henry snoring away, clueless to the miracle. I could tell he was trying to control his legs and arms in a way that would make it seem a more natural gait, but there would be time for all that. Time and practice.

Perhaps, eventually, dramatic surgery of a sort. Bones realigned? Limbs turned?

My god, but the possibilities were endless!

—

My plan was a simple one:

Careful, respectful, suffocation.

Martin and I discussed it over a series of nights, his eyes now bright and alert, his features more fully-formed on the back of Henry's skull.

Henry, meanwhile, had begun to suffer some side effects.

His vision, for one, became problematic. I remember the day he came home, bleeding from the forehead. Shaken and crying.

I was immediately afraid for Martin and made a point to study the back of Henry's head for cuts or contusions. Martin's face was not evident, having disappeared to wherever he went off to when he didn't want to be seen, but neither were there any injuries to speak of.

"I told you, honey, it's just my forehead," he said, and I *tsked* and bothered and got him a cold cloth to put on it. I sat him at the kitchen table and held his hand. When he looked up at me I must have gasped, because it got him crying again. "Something's wrong with me!" he yelled.

And there was.

Henry's blue eyes had begun to fade.

"I don't know if it's a disease or what, but suddenly I can't see worth shit and when I look in the mirror I get scared as hell," he said, weeping so terribly that I felt a pang of remorse for the man,

95

the way you might feel badly for a stranger who gets hit by a car, or a child who falls off a cliff. "I think I need to see a doctor, sweetheart."

I wiped the blood from his forehead and stroked his stubbled head. "I don't know if that would help. I mean...do you?" I said, trying not to act alarmed, as if my husband's eyes turning ghost-white was the equivalent of a stomach ache, like he was mistaking indigestion for a heart attack. "Maybe we wait a few days and see if it goes away, whatever it is."

"That's not all of it," he said, whimpering. "I mean, my vision going is bad enough. I didn't even see the damn road was out until I was steering the car into a ditch. Two city workers had to pull me free and call a tow truck. I was so shaken I just left the car there and walked the rest of the way. But lately I'm feeling like I can't breathe so good, and all my joints hurt. Arthritis or something. But I'm not even forty years old! How the hell can I have arthritis? And what...from one day to the next? Dammit, Liv, I was brushing my teeth yesterday morning and one of the darned things fell out!"

He tilted his head toward me and lifted a lip with his finger to show me the hole where a low incisor should have rooted. It was gruesome, all right. Gave me a chill, to be honest, seeing him fall apart like that.

"I don't mind saying it, Liv. I'm scared. I'm thinking...well hell...might as well just say it. I think maybe I got cancer or something."

"No, baby, no," I said soothingly, and hugged his head to my chest, knowing breasts make men forget just about anything. "You don't have cancer and a loose tooth doesn't mean a thing. What you need, my love, is a good night's rest. As a matter of fact," I said, reaching behind me and handing him the drink I'd prepared when I saw him stumbling up the driveway, "why don't you have a drink and go lie down. I think what you need, Henry, is to sleep."

After a few minutes of him drinking and crying, I finally got him up and walked him to the bedroom, where I took off his boots and jeans, tucked him beneath a blanket.

I sat cross-legged at the foot of the bed and waited until he snored.

These days I didn't need to push his body around to accommodate Martin. He could do it just fine by himself.

Henry's body rolled over and he snorted and coughed, then resumed his blissful snoring. I looked up to see Martin watching me, a sadness in his eyes that nearly broke my heart.

"I don't like seeing him like this," I said.

Martin nodded, reached a hand around to scratch his nose lightly. "No, I don't either, Olivia. I think..." he started, then lowered his eyes, as if ashamed.

And that was okay. It was my task to complete. He was, after all, *my* husband.

"Yes," I said. "It's almost time."

—

"What the hell are you doing?"

"What? Oh..." I stared at the drink as if it held a good answer. A believable response.

I hadn't expected Henry to leave the bedroom. The last few days I'd been bringing him meals in bed, along with a heavily-dosed drink. Not enough to kill him, but enough to keep him sleeping most of the day, and all of the night.

His condition, I'm afraid, had deteriorated.

After the car accident, he'd called in sick to work, told them he'd been hurt and needed time to recover before returning to the warehouse. A week, at least. Perhaps more. In the days that followed his vision grew worse, his breathing labored. He lost two more teeth. His face had grown first ashen, then jaundiced. And while his facial hair had been allowed to grow, I'd taken it upon myself to— carefully, mind you, *oh so carefully*—shave the rest of his head bald.

Seeing Martin, clearly, for the first time nearly took my breath away.

His skin smooth (with the exception of those delicate black eyebrows), his eyes vibrant and alive, his mouth full and cherry-lipped, his nose perfect. There was one moment when he actually *sneezed!* We both went wide-eyed in shock before laughing wildly. How joyous that sneeze had been. I think even Henry, in some fashion, was aware that something strange and wonderful had occurred, for he started mumbling in his sleep, or stupor if you prefer, since he was hardly ever fully-conscious anymore.

So, as you can imagine, when Henry came stumbling into the kitchen and saw me pouring the powder of three crushed tablets into his iced tea, it was quite, as I said, unexpected. It also left me with some explaining to do. His weakened vision, apparently, was not as poor as I'd surmised. *Mon erreur.*

"Darling, it's sleeping pills. Here, look," and I showed him the prescription bottle. After all, he was sick, I said. Terribly ill. He needed his rest.

His anger became stupefaction, and then turned completely into horrific despair. It was heartbreaking, to be honest, as he started to weep openly there in the kitchen, saying over and over how scared he was. "Am I dying?" he said, and asked again for the hospital.

"But Henry, you have no insurance." This was true. "How could we ever pay for something like that? Better to wait, dear, to wait and see if you can recover on your own, with rest and proper nutrition."

He looked at me, his horrible chalky eyes wet and red-rimmed. "Recover?" he stammered. "I can hardly see! My fucking teeth are falling out. I struggle to breathe. My mind..." He stopped then, as if finding the right words, like an ass bobbing for apples in a rain-filled barrel, "is muddled," he finished. "I don't know dream from reality, and...it's crazy, but I hear voices. I hear someone else in my head, talking as if...as if..."

I embraced him as he broke down. I didn't want him to suffer any further, and although I'd hoped to postpone the inevitable, I knew, just as Martin had said a few days prior, that it was time to end things. To move on with my life. Open a new door.

My heart hammered with the thrill of it.

"Let's get you to bed," I said.

And that's when things went a little crazy.

"Bed!" he screamed, and pushed me away with

such force that I rammed into the kitchen table, knocking over a chair and disrupting a bowl of apples I'd picked up at the market for Martin and me. One rolled off and thumped to the floor, likely bruising.

Then Henry was on me.

His large hands were curled, claw-like, as they reached for me. "It's YOU!" he roared, clutching my fragile neck and gripping it so tightly I gasped, then gagged.

*He's gone mad!* I thought, terrified.

"You're doing this," he continued, pushing me back and down onto the table with his brutish hands. My dress fell to the waist, my bare legs kicking the air, trying to find purchase against him as he raised me by the neck then *slammed* me hard against the tabletop, knocking the remaining breath from my lungs. "I don't know how, or...or WHY!" he screamed, and his face sagged, as if he'd suffered a horrible stroke and all the muscles had slackened into useless dead sinew. "Why would you do this to me?" he sobbed, his tears spilling onto my face. "I love you..." Then his face tightened once more...and his hands began to *squeeze.*

"Enough!"

Henry's eyes went wide with a sort of shocked horror. His fingers snapped open, releasing my throat. I breathed in glorious air and hacked as his body straightened, his eyes wild with confusion. "What's happening…" he stuttered, and then Martin's voice came again.

"Now, Olivia!" he yelled.

"Who…what the hell is that!" Henry screeched, his bland gray irises darting left and right in search of the voice, the one he could not fathom was coming from his own thick head.

Jerkily, as if pulled by invisible strings, Henry began to stumble away, toward the hallway which led to our bedroom.

He was walking backwards.

"Liv! Help me!" Henry cried out, as if suddenly dismissing the fact he was—only moments ago—trying to choke me to death!

His body spun savagely; he squealed like a stabbed pig and I saw his crotch darken as he pissed himself. It was now Martin who looked at me, stared at me with haunted, desperate eyes. "Are you ready?" he asked. "Can you do this?"

I nodded, breathless, and followed him quietly down the hallway as he led my husband's body to its death. I paused only once, just outside the doorway, steeling my nerves. *You can do this,* I thought, knowing there would be no turning back. *It isn't even murder! Not technically…* The body, the mind, the very soul...all of that would survive! So how could it be wrong? How could any of it be wrong?

When I stepped into the bedroom Henry lay face down on the bed, legs straight as fenceposts, arms glued to his sides, face buried in a pillow. Martin dared not move his head, but his eyes darted to me. "I can control him for a while, but he's still strong, Olivia. There's a battle of wills going on here that you cannot see, so please, for us, for our love, for our future...*HURRY!*"

I climbed onto the mattress, crawled over to the body and straddled it like I had on so many nights previous; but this time there was nothing sexual to the act, and instead of looking at the Janus head of two faces, one asleep and quiet, the other alert and aroused, I was looking only at Martin.

"I don't have the strength," he whispered. "You need to *push*. Put your hands..."

"I know darling," I said, and without another moment's hesitation I pressed my palms against the sides of his head, leaned all my weight forward.

Henry's muffled cries were so distant as to be almost indistinguishable. The sounds could have been practically anything! A television or a radio left on in another room. Someone having a conversation outside my window. Children playing. A dog barking from the backyard of a neighbor's home.

"Shut up!" I yelled, my mouth stretching into a rictus-grin as pure elation surged through my body, the hot pleasure of murder. "Shut up, you DOG!"

Martin's eyes never left my own; his smile horribly stretched by the force of pressure I was exerting, but it seemed genuine, and warm. Grateful.

Henry's protests turned to gurgles, and then, blissfully, silence. Martin's eyelids lowered slightly, and he seemed to be gasping for breath.

"Martin! My love!" I shrieked. *Oh mon Dieu! Had I killed them both?*

A hand came up and beat against my leg, gently through, as if in signal. I think, had Martin been able to reach his own head from that position, he would have pulled my hands away. Sadly, the elbow joints prevented this, but I understood the message:

*Enough.*

*He's dead.*

*Enough.*

With a wet gasp I removed my hands, bunched them into anxious fists and held them to my belly.

I watched in horror as Martin seemed to choke; his eyelids fluttered, his skin reddened.

And then, as if witnessing the birth of a beautiful child, his eyes shot wide with euphoric LIFE, his nostrils flared and his mouth opened like a pulled cork, a soft *pop* emanated as lips parted and he pulled in a large gasp of air, then released it.

Pulled it in, released.

He was breathing on his own.

He was finally, truly, *alive.*

"Martin!" I said and kissed him.

And for the first time in his life he wept. Tears of joy.

"He's gone," he said quietly, his smile touching in its delicacy, not gloating but relieved. Thankful for the sacrifice others made so that he might live. "He's really gone, and I...the body...it's *me."*

"Yes, yes, darling," I whimpered into his ear.

Finally, love had found a way.

—

The next couple weeks were like a dream.

Martin and I spent every minute together. Talking and loving and *living* as a couple—a *real* couple—at all hours of the day, not just at night anymore, like some illicit affair.

We discussed our future. I wanted to travel— Paris! Rome! London! He looked forward to a new wardrobe, taking ownership of his tastes and personality.

Of course, there were small setbacks, as with any new relationship. In our case, however, many of the issues to figure out were physical, rather than, say, philosophical.

Chairs, for example.

But Martin quickly found that turning our kitchen chairs around and straddling them backwards was as fine as any manner of sitting. The fact that all of his joints were locked in odd directions made mealtimes strange, but I quickly grew used to the way he'd hold the plate up high, just below the neck, and shovel the food in without too much spillage.

He became adept at moving around the house, and everyday things like using the toilet or brushing teeth became natural almost overnight.

There was one larger issue, though, which was Henry.

Or, more pointedly, Henry's face.

The first couple days Henry's features... well...sort of *melted*. I honestly don't know another way to put it. His lips smeared together as if they'd been glued, or stitched, shut. His nostrils narrowed, growing slimmer until they, too, sealed into one patch of lumpy skin. The cartilage of his nose seemingly, I don't know...*dissolved* I guess, leaving a rather unattractive, flabby bump that sort of bobbed and jiggled whenever Martin moved, creating a horrible distraction during our frequent, and heated, lovemaking.

His eyes, though, were the worst.

Unlike the mouth and nose, the eyelids would not seal, despite my efforts with first fingers, then glue and, desperately, heavy tape. The eyeballs had liquified, you see, and would drip down what were once Henry's strong-boned cheeks like milky tears. They leaked onto the bed, or from beneath the tape during a meal, or when trying to relax on the couch with a couple books (it turned out Martin *loved* reading almost as much as I—no surprise, of course).

Regardless, after the first week the leaking eyes finally stopped, and I used a needle-and-thread to sew the lids firmly closed.

"Martin," I asked as I stitched, "how would you feel about a wig?"

He looked at me, seemingly caught off guard, then, after a moment's reflection, nodded. "I suppose it doesn't bother me the way it must you, my dear. Seeing Henry like that."

"Oh, please, let's not say his name. But, in truth, yes, it can be...unsettling."

He agreed at once and the very next morning I went back to the beauty supply store for options. I ended up fitting a wonderful, well-coiffed jet-black toupee onto Martin's head that quite neatly covered the odd landscape of bumps, stitches and facial hair of Henry's dead visage.

After combing it to my taste, I followed Martin into the bathroom where he admired his new head of hair. Admittedly, it looked strange at first because Martin himself had neglected to shave over the last day or so, so the total, immediate, affect was a bit barbaric. Once he'd shaven his own skin clear, however, he looked handsome as the devil himself.

And so, finally, all traces of Henry were forever erased.

Life could go on.

—

Sadly, Life turned out to be an intrusive, problematic bitch.

But what do we expect from true love? It is, after all, just a feeling. It's not *real*. You can't sell it, or breathe it, or eat it. And it's feral, I think. A wild thing let loose from a cage. Two people perhaps, together, *think* they can tame it, control it.

But I don't believe it's possible, do you?

As much as one could control a full-grown tiger

in their kitchen, their living room, their bedroom—even if well-behaved, the animal still has teeth and claws, a sense of freedom so powerful it will gladly tear you limb-from-limb to enforce its desire, its heart-stamped will.

So, for a few weeks, Martin and I lived happily. The tiger, to further the analogy, was controlled; docile and beautiful and warm. Love could be cuddled and held. Revered.

There came a day, however, another hot summer afternoon, when I could almost see the great cat pacing, dark rumbles percolating from its chest, gnashing its great teeth in annoyance, gouging walls and furniture with its claws.

Love and Life were at odds.

And though Love is fierce, it is Life which holds the whip.

—

Bills began to pile up, and things around the house grew tense.

"Me?" I exclaimed one night over drinks in the living room, the fireplace roaring and things cozy and romantic, right up until the topic of money was raised. "Work? Doing what, Martin? I mean...my God!"

"Well, darling, see the sense of it," he said, infuriatingly calm. "I have certain...setbacks. For me to enter the workplace would take some ingenuity, to say the least. I fear I'd be seen more as a liability than an asset in most business settings, be they industrial or clerical. I can't bend and lift too well and, frankly, writing or using a keyboard would cause me fits. I have to see what I'm doing, don't I?"

I saw his point, and wondered why I'd never thought about it until now. Of *course* we would need money. Without Henry's income from the warehouse there was absolutely nothing with which to pay the bills, and (although I hadn't mentioned it to Martin) the credit cards I'd been using to stock the house with groceries, booze, and the many beauty supply store needs were all but maxed-out.

We were broke.

"If only..." I said in a sigh, knowing damn well what I was doing. If I couldn't get him to see reason, I'd use jealousy against him. There were a hundred ways to spur a man to action, most of which meant digging your heels into their damn backsides.

"Only what?" he said, then smirked. It looked ugly on him, and it wasn't an expression I'd seen before. "Oh, I see. If only *Henry* were still here, is that it? Old Henry, sure, he could lift things, and sit face-forward in a chair, and screw you while looking into your eyes instead of at a pillow, is that it?"

"My gosh, Martin, I didn't say that at all! And I certainly wasn't thinking such things!"

I was, of course.

Martin stood from the chair and began pacing in that strange, backward way of his, wringing his hands in front of him—just above his rump.

"Well, hell," he said, and I could tell I'd upset him more than I intended. "I don't know what to say, or do for that matter. Maybe...maybe it would be better if I just left."

I jumped to my feet and ran to him. I knew he was manipulating me just as much as I was him, but I didn't care. For him to even suggest such a thing brought me to tears.

"No, please! Don't even say it!" I yelled, kissing his round chin, his fuzzy neck, stroking the hair which felt so close to natural. "I'm sorry! I'm being selfish. I'll find something. A secretary, perhaps. Or a librarian."

Martin smiled down at me. "There are many other jobs, Olivia. You could go back to school, really make something of yourself. You'd like that, wouldn't you? To be smarter? More well-equipped for the real world?"

I didn't care for this line of thought, and I didn't much care for the way he was looking at me when he said it. I got the impression he was not saying it to me at all, but to someone else. Someone who wasn't even there.

—

I did end up getting a job and was soon leaving early every morning to work as a salesperson in a local dress shop—ironically, the very one I liked to frequent, despite my inability to afford any of the fashions. As it turned out, I *enjoyed* the work. Took pride in providing for our home, for our lives. It was tiring, certainly, and customers could take their toll on one after a while, but overall it was fulfilling and, if I can be frank, nice to be away from Martin now and then. He never left the house, you see. And. in his lethargy, he had put on some weight. Henry had always been thin and well-toned, strong from all the days of lifting heavy boxes and working on his feet for hours on end, but Martin didn't lift anything at all, and the only time he was on his feet was when he walked from one end of the house to the other.

When we did see each other, he would go on and on about whatever book of science or philosophy he'd been reading that day, espousing theories and histories of ancient men that was so tiresome and dull it was all I could do not to scream and run from the room in search of hard liquor.

Still, relationships are work, aren't they? Sure they are. You have to keep at it and toil through the problems that arise day-to-day, week-to-week. And I still thought, all-in-all, that we got on quite well together. I certainly believed we had a bright future ahead of us.

It seemed Martin did, as well. It was he who suggested we renew our wedding vows. When he told me, I squealed and hugged him at the idea of having a new ceremony, just for us. We already had the rings, of course, and technically I was no widow—not really—but it seemed wildly appropriate for us to commit to the *new* couple. Martin and Olivia, forever.

Or so I thought.

For weeks after his suggestion, however, Martin acted peculiar. For one thing, he kept putting off the date of the ceremony, claiming we should "give it a bit more time" whenever I brought it up for discussion.

I also believed he'd been leaving the house. Nothing more than a hunch, really, but upon my return from work I'd notice his shoes by the door, the soles sometimes clumped with fresh dirt. One night, while he slept, I hunted through the pockets of his pants and coats and found strange items: a matchbook from a nearby pub (an establishment I knew Henry hated and wouldn't be caught dead in), a pen engraved with the name of a local motel, and, most oddly of all, a parking stub. Why, the very thought of Martin driving anywhere was ridiculous, unless he made the whole trip in reverse!

Still, it was disquieting, and mysterious.

I didn't become truly alarmed, however, until a few nights ago. Martin must have thought I was asleep, but with my back turned to him he probably couldn't have known for sure. Regardless, my eyes were closed and I was breathing steadily enough, but my mind was tangled with the threads of Martin and the strange discoveries, my dancing suspicions. I suppose I was lightly dozing, or perhaps in the process of sinking into a deeper sleep, because I was confused at first as to what I was hearing.

Soft sounds from behind me. Pleading whispers, spoken so quietly as to be no louder than a heavy breath. But as I rose to full consciousness, full awareness, I could make out words:

*...don't worry...soon...I love you...I know, I know...be patient, my love...*

I cleared my throat heavily and his words abruptly stopped. I turned my head to say something, but he was asleep, or feigning to be. His lips moved as he slept, and I think he might have been dreaming, talking in his sleep. Perhaps even talking to a dream version of me. I liked the idea of that, and forced myself to relax, drift away to my own dreams.

When I woke the next morning, I hardly recalled the incident, and kissed him with passion as I made my way out the door. I turned back only once—just as I was about to get into the car—to blow him one last kiss, tell him how much I loved him.

He was waving when I turned, a lustful smile on his face that turned, momentarily, to chagrin. Then he rebounded and continued to wave, smiling wide.

"Goodbye, my love," he said, and it became he who blew the kiss, and me who caught it.

—

I think I knew the truth of it now. And the horror.

Earlier this evening, after dinner, Martin brought me a glass of wine. Within an hour of drinking it, I felt woozy and tired, as if my entire body had turned to lead, and my head to thick cotton.

115

"You look tired, my love," he said, and guided me to the bedroom. "Why don't you get some sleep. I think you need it."

"But it's not even seven o'clock," I protested childishly. "The sun's not fully set." I pointed to the bedroom window, where a hazy red sky was bruising violet.

He cocked his head, as if thinking, and took my hands in his. He recited an old poem I'd never heard: "In the gloaming, oh, my darling, think not bitterly of me. Though I passed away in silence; left you lonely, set you free."

"That's beautiful," I said, and thought my words might have slurred just a bit.

"I agree. It's from a poem Henry read while a freshman in college. I'll get you her book, if you'd like. Now, off to bed with you. Come, dear."

"Yes," I said, and let him undress me completely, then cover me with a cool, thin sheet. I lay there thinking about Henry, tried to picture him as a young man, reading a poem in a classroom. I felt a sharp pang of unforeseen sorrow, but it wilted like a dying flower, and I slept.

—

I must have dozed a while, because when I wake it is pitch dark, and I can sense Martin lying in the bed next to me, though my back is turned to him.

He is whispering again.

I try to ignore him, to push down the stab of fear that cuts through my heart.

I feel suddenly overwhelmed with guilt; a deep, bottomless sorrow of regret for what I did to dear Henry. How awful that it came to murder, for that's what it was.

What I was, deep-down.

All I ever wanted was a nice dress. A trip to somewhere far away. Love—*true* love—that I know exists in other parts of the world, with other people; people who are much more real than I am.

And now, as Martin whispers, I let the guilt have its way with me. Truth be told it's well-deserved. Besides, it serves as a distraction from the true terror—what I am right now, this moment, trying so desperately to ignore:

The intense itching rampant along my scalp, the odd sensation of the skin on the back of my head being pulled and misaligned—as if by the opening of delicate white eyes, or the upturned lips of a loving smile.

¤

Eleonore began to whine as the lights of town faded behind them. Everything was wrong and this driver... She dialled her son once more.

Tobias had his arms folded over his chest and was frowning, his eyes were bloodshot and his cheeks were puffy and pink. "Where in the fuck are we going? Pull over. Pull over now, you inbred hick!"

The driver kept his attention forward while his meaty right hand fidgeted with the threads atop his head. A small gap had formed and something black jutted out and hid before Eleonore could be sure she saw it. She leaned away, just in case, nearly sitting in her husband's lap. The cellphone rang and rang in her ear.

"There it is," the driver said. "Like opening a rice bag, you know?"

"You pull this...!" Tobias began screaming.

A click sounded as the line connected in Eleonore's ear. "Ross? Ross? Are you...?"

"Mom?" Ross shouted. "Mom, how...?"

"...fucking truck over...!" Tobias yanked the door handle.

"...okay? My baby...?" Eleonore was so relieved she felt like fainting.

The driver sighed in pleasure. "That's better." He tossed the thread with a wrist flick. It splatted wetly against the interior of the windshield. Gooey. Pink. Nasty.

"...are you doing this?" Ross was crying.

"...right now or I'll have you charged...!" Tobias continued to swing his finger at the driver.

"...tell me—doing what?" Eleonore stiffened, side-eyeing the driver. His bald scalp seemed to rattle atop his head.

"...with kidnapping and criminal...!" Tobias leaned over his wife, pointing a finger next to the driver's right ear, unnoticing of the motion at the top of his head.

"Mom, how are you talking to me?" Tears bubbled around Ross' words.

"...mischief and assault...!" Tobias spat as he screamed.

"My cell, my—" Eleonore was crying and her words snagged in her throat as if caught on a nail when Ross yelled.

"No, but you're dead! You and Dad are dead!" Ross wailed into the phone. "I can hear him! But you're dead! Dead!"

"...and that's just for—ah!" Tobias screamed as the stub where his index finger had been only a heartbeat prior pumped blood like a tiny geyser. He grabbed for the door handle to find that it no longer existed.

"No. No. Nonononononono!" Eleonore buried her face in her husband's chest, a chest that vibrated with the steady scream.

The roof of the driver's head popped off and landed on the dash, rolling like a wooden bowl. Twelve tiny gremlins—black with bright orange, beady eyes, four razor sharp claws on each hand, long shark-like snouts and shark-like teeth— moved fluidly as a sea streaming down the driver's shoulder. The leader leapt from Tobias' hand. Tobias was screaming and shaking the absence of a finger. Eleonore screamed at the sight of it.

The lead gremlin spat the cleaned bones as it charged up Eleonore's thigh. The others were spreading, fanning out, finding thighs and arms...meat.

"You're dead, Mom! You're dead!" Ross shouted, his voice clear and biting, even as the cellphone fell to the floor of the truck.

The driver continued driving, the Enfields continued screaming, and the gremlins dined little bits at a time.

REWIND OR DIE

# REWIND OR DIE

Midnight Exhibit Vol. 1
Infested - Carol Gore
Benny Rose: The Cannibal King - Hailey Piper - Jan. 23
Cirque Berserk - Jessica Guess - Feb. 20
Hairspray and Switchblades - V. Castro - Feb. 20
Sole Survivor - Zachary Ashford - Mar. 26
Food Fright - Nico Bell - Mar. 26
Hell's Bells - Lisa Quigley - May 28
The Kelping - Jan Stinchcomb - May 28
Trampled Crown - Kirby Kellogg - Jun. 25
Dead and Breakfast - Gary Buller - Jun. 25
Blood Lake Monster - Renee Miller - Jul. 23
The Catcatcher - Kevin Lewis - Jul. 23
All You Need is Love and a Strong Electric Current -
Mackenzie Kiera - Aug. 27
Tales From the Meat Wagon - Eddie Generous - Aug. 27
Hooker - M. Lopes da Silva - Oct. 29
Offstage Offerings - Priya Sridhar - Oct. 29
Dead Eyes - EV Knight - Nov. 26
Dancing on the Edge of a Blade - Todd Rigney - Dec. 12
Midnight Exhibit Vol. 2 - Dec. 12

www.UNNERVINGMAGAZINE.com

Printed in Great Britain
by Amazon